WHEN ART Falls

LIVING IN CIN

LORRAIN ALLEN

GW00659950

Edited by: Emily Hainsworth
http://www.emilyhainsworth.com

Proofread by: Maggie Kern
https://www.facebook.com/Ms.Kedits

Proofread by: Novel Nurse Editing
https://NovelNurseEditing.com/

Formatted by: Brenda Wright
https://www.facebook.com/FormattingDoneWright/

Author's Note

This book features an out-of-control, jealous antihero, abuse, graphic language, explicit sex scenes, and other subject matters some readers might find triggering. Arthur King is not a comfortable antihero to read about. If you expect a redeemable antihero this book is not for you. He does NOT grovel or beg. Scan QR code to view content warning.

Playlist

"When We" – Tank
"When We Remix" – Tank featuring Trey Songz & Ty Dolla Sign
"Hurts Too Good" – Ruelle
War Of Hearts" – Ruelle
"Never Be The Same" – Camila Cabello
"Bad Things" – Machine Gun Kelly & Camila Cabello
"Set Fire To The Rain" – Adele
"The Heart Wants What It Wants" – Selena Gomez
"Desire" – Meg Myers
"Flesh" – Simon Curtis
"Going Under" – Evanescence
"We Found Love" – Rihanna featuring Calvin Harris

Prologue

ART

"Where are you going?"

I look over and see the old man approaching as I climb on my motorcycle. "I'll meet you in Boston."

"You shouldn't drive in your current state."

I rev the engine before speeding off.

You should've died the day you slit your wrists.

Those words echo in my mind nonstop. The first person I gave my heart to and trusted implicitly destroyed the bright future I saw looming ahead of me, but damn if I don't still want her.

You pussy-whipped moron.

I'm a fucking idiot for putting so much faith in a girl who wasn't loyal to her boyfriend. I gave her the power to mortally wound me. Damn her to hell for making me believe in something I thought would forever be out of my reach. I'll have my revenge against her if it's the last thing I do. I don't care how long it takes. I'll finally relent and follow in the old man's footsteps, becoming the emotionless narcissistic robot he always wanted to mold me into without allowing him complete dominance over me. He'll know who's really in charge. I'll succeed where my father failed. As for the opposite sex, they'll only be used to sate my carnal needs, then be discarded like trash.

Lightning cracks across the sky, matching my turbulent mood. I travel down the road, oblivious to my surroundings. The heavy rain comes next, completely soaking me. I have a fucking death wish, so instead of slowing down like any sane person would, I press on the throttle until I hit maximum speed. I refuse to pull over if the sheriff or Deputy These Nuts gives chase. I'm a fucked-up rich white boy with a chip on my shoulder, mad at the damn world. Today the beast is born. Art no longer exists. I learned the hard way that nothing good can ever come from living a life of "Cin."

One

Eight years later

Cin

I stand in the doorway of my new apartment, catching my breath. I'm exhausted from lugging boxes up six flights of stairs for the last hour. The building itself has ten floors. I would have preferred an apartment on the first level, but no vacancies were available. Not one elevator in the building is operational, but I was assured by the property manager that repairs would be happening very soon. At least I don't live on the top floor. Boy, do I feel sorry for the people who do. The outdated high-rise looks as if it should be scheduled for demolition. I lucked out and was able to rent one of the last subsidized apartments available, so I am grateful because there's no way I could afford market rent. The one-bedroom apartment with a den is small, but it fits my budget. Sebastian and I will share the bedroom while my mom uses the den as hers. I plan to save money so Mom can start seeing specialists again. Trying to accomplish that while paying off student loans and monthly bills will be hard. To top it off, I need a new car.

"Move it, old woman." Anneli knees me in the butt. "These boxes are heavy."

I step to the side. "Watch it, asshole."

"Mommy said a bad word!" Sebastian jumps up and down.

Anneli covers her mouth in mock horror. "Sebastian, go tell your grandmother your mom said a bad word."

"Grandma!" He races from the apartment before I can stop him.

"Not only are you an asshole, you're a bitch too."

"Is that any way to speak to your best friend who's spending her first Saturday off in weeks helping you settle in?" She places a box on the kitchen counter.

Anneli is always there for me. After the debacle, my popularity vanished overnight and I became a pariah. She remained my best friend, despite being bullied for it. I practically lived at her house. Being terrorized every damn day took a toll on me, but I refused to drop out of school. I stopped eating, sleeping, and even quit the track team. Trevor made sure everyone knew I was a cheating slut, and Josh, a jealous prick. Needless to say, their friendship ended after Art spilled the beans. There was no more Chaos and our little group disbanded, taking sides. I chose not to attend prom or graduation. My mind wanders to those last dark months in North Carolina on occasion, though I try to keep it from straying there. Mom and I left on the last day of school. We went back to Phoenix and never looked back. Anneli and I kept in touch after she moved to Florida in pursuit of a nursing degree. We visited each other a few times over the years, but not for a long time.

"Cin, are you listening to me?"

"I'm sorry. What did you say?"

"I know what that blank stare means."

She knows all too well.

"You went back there again."

"Yeah." I walk over to the sofa to sit down.

Anneli joins me. "You have to forgive yourself."

"I ruined so many lives that day because of my selfishness."

The impact from the boot Trevor threw ruptured my mom's left eye, causing her to lose sight. She sports a glass eye or sometimes wears a patch. She has severe migraines several times a week that prevent her from functioning, and maintaining employment. Doctors are baffled, unable to provide a diagnosis, and labeled her condition a medical mystery. But my mom's not the only one who suffered that night because of me. Josh lost his scholarship and dream of becoming a professional football player. His fall over the banister crushed the tibia and fibula in his lower right leg. Josh had emergency surgery the next day. Doctors put a titanium rod in his tibia, with four screws just below his kneecap and right above his ankle. I don't know who hated me more—Art, Trevor, or Josh. Ricky and my mom's engagement ended over the incident. I'll never forgive myself for ruining her chance at happiness. They both agreed it was better if they no longer worked together. He was generous enough to give Mom a severance package of two months' salary. Of course, that wasn't enough to sustain us, so we had no other choice but to move in with Aunt Katrina. When Mom's health insurance ended, the doctor visits stopped and she could no longer see the specialists to find an answer regarding her migraines. She forgave me instantly and has never shown the tiniest bit of resentment.

"I'm not in the mood to have this conversation again."

"Well, that's too damn bad."

"I'm tired. It's been a really long day."

We stayed the night at Anneli's after arriving in Orlando yesterday evening. I drove the moving truck while Mom drove my beat-up old car from Phoenix. I'm honestly surprised it withstood the journey. I thought it would be fun for Sebastian to experience his first road trip, and I wanted one last hurrah before we started the next chapter in our lives. We checked into a few dingy motels and did some sightseeing along the way. The thirty-plus–hour drive was exhausting, but the memories we created are priceless. My mind wanders back to another road trip with a haunted green-eyed boy. The car I had at the time was a piece of shit too.

Art and Josh have been featured on tabloid news shows and magazine covers, being two of America's youngest billionaires. I'm assuming they forgave each other and joined their grandfather in expanding the Falcon hotel chain, where only the rich and famous can afford to stay. Art was out of control, arrested several times for drug possession, DUIs, disorderly conduct, and a host of other charges, but for the last few years he's remained out of the limelight. I hope he's doing a lot better. I'm still devastated he thinks I betrayed him. I have no idea who told his secret, but it sure as hell wasn't me.

"You're coming out with me tonight."

"I absolutely will not."

"When are you going to free yourself from this self-induced prison?"

Never

"When was the last time you had sex?"

Three years ago. "Last month."

"Liar."

"I'm not lying," I sputter.

"With whom?"

"Some random guy I met at a bar. It was a one-off."

Anneli snorts. "You expect me to believe you?"

"Why would I lie?"

"Well, you never mentioned it during any of our weekly calls."

"It slipped my mind."

"Ha!"

"Cinnamon!" I hear my mom yell.

I glance towards the open door. She's calling me by my full name, which means I'm in deep shit.

"You started this," I accuse.

"Hey, you're the one who said the bad word."

My mom appears in the doorway, her hands on her hips, ready to lay into me. The little tattletale peers under her arm with a self-satisfied look on his face.

"Are you using the devil's language in front of my grandchild?"

I point at Anneli. "It's her fault."

Mom walks over, then whacks me across the back of my head.

"Ouch."

"If you use another bad word around my grandchild, I'll wash your mouth out with soap."

"I'm sorry, jeez."

"Good. It's nearly noon and my baby hasn't had lunch yet."

"Grandma, I'm not a baby," Sebastian protests.

"You are absolutely right, big boy." She grasps his cheeks, placing a kiss on his forehead.

"Yuck!" He pulls away from her.

She pops him on the butt. "That's a million-dollar kiss, boy. I'm going to use the bathroom, then I'll make you something to eat."

Once the door closes, I turn to Sebastian. "You know snitches get stitches, right?"

"Grandma! Grandma!" He hightails it towards the bathroom.

I look heavenwards. He always runs to his grandmother for protection.

Anneli laughs. "Sebastian, I have a special treat for you."

He changes direction as quick as a whip and comes to a stop in front of Anneli, holding out his hand.

Spoiled brat.

"You owe me one." She winks.

"No, we're even. You're the reason I'm in this mess to begin with."

She hands Sebastian a candy bar from her bag.

"Thank you, Auntie Anneli!"

"You're welcome. Now beat it, kiddo."

Sebastian runs off with his treat.

I lean back against the couch cushions.

"He looks just like his dad," Anneli says.

"I know."

That's why it pains me to look at him sometimes.

I decided not to tell Trevor about my pregnancy while still living in North Carolina because I was afraid of his reaction. He became this person I didn't recognize after we broke up. I waited until relocating out west before reaching out to him. Of course, he called me all types of horrible names and denied being the father, which is understandable since I wasn't sure myself. I thought it best not to contact Art unless Trevor was proven not to be the father. But there was no doubt in my mind who Sebastian belonged to after I gave birth and looked into his bright blue eyes—the same as Trevor's. I filed for a paternity test through family court because he refused to go on his own. I learned Trevor ended up attending college in California after all, so we were able to meet at a DNA laboratory in Los Angeles. It broke my heart when he looked at our baby boy in disgust. Trevor was proven to be Sebastian's father. I thought his hate for me wouldn't prevent him from wanting a relationship with his son, but he made it clear he and his family wanted nothing to do with us. I didn't stop him from walking away, nor did I demand he provide financial assistance for Sebastian.

"Okay, it's time to check out your wardrobe." Anneli leaves the sofa.

"Why?"

"Because we're hitting the streets tonight whether you want to or not." She sashays into my bedroom.

"Anneli," I say on a long-suffering sigh.

"Hush. We're going, and that's final."

"You're not the boss of me!" I yell.

She sticks her head out the door. "I'm totally boss of you."

It looks like the next chapter of my life is going to be really exciting.

Cin

"Can you at least pretend to be excited?" Anneli asks as she maneuvers her car through traffic.

I turn from watching the drunken tourists make spectacles of themselves to peer at her. "No."

Once Anneli told my mom about her plans to take me to a bar tonight, they both nagged me nonstop until I agreed to go for at least an hour.

"If you think I'm going to let you stay cooped up in your apartment all the time, you've lost your mind. You live in the Sunshine State now, where all the beautiful people are."

"I thought California is where all the beautiful people are."

"All the plastic people you mean."

"Are you sure about that? I spotted several women whose breasts looked hard as rocks."

"Okay, maybe half the plastic people live here. But you, my dear, are among the beautiful, so you're going to have to dress like it."

"What's wrong with my outfit?"

"Is that a trick question?"

"I'm very stylish."

"Oh no, you poor foolish thing. You are absolutely clueless. Turn your attention back out the window."

My eyes scan the crowd of people. "What am I looking for?"

"Do you see anyone dressed similarly to you at all?"

"Well, not everyone can pull this off." I rub my hands down my big bright orange polo shirt and loose-fitting cargo shorts.

"Yep, including you. We're going on a shopping spree as soon as possible."

"I can't afford it."

"No worries. I'll foot the bill. Pay me back when you can."

"You've already done more than enough for me."

I wouldn't have been offered the health and physical education teacher position without the glowing recommendation she gave to the principal of Westbrook High School, who also happens to be her boyfriend's sister. I'm taking on the responsibility of assistant track and field coach as well. I start in three weeks. The high school is almost an hour drive from the apartment. It took a while, but I finally graduated with a bachelor's degree in the spring. Mom and I moved in with Dad's mother after relocating back to Phoenix. I thought it was going to be a disaster since they never got along when my mom and dad were together, but they were cordial towards one another. By the time Sebastian was born, Dad had remarried. He chose to spend all his time and money on his new family, not offering me a cent for my college education—much to Mom's and my grandmother's dismay. I opted to take part-time classes at a nearby community college and worked to help my grandmother with monthly expenses so we wouldn't be a financial burden on her. Mom felt useless and continued to apply for jobs, only to be terminated within a month from the few positions she was offered. She was stuck between a rock and a hard place. The state wouldn't approve free healthcare or public assistance for her, ruling she was fit to work.

"It's no problem, Cin—"

"I'm not a charity case, so would you drop it already?"

"Fine."

She's only given me a reprieve. More than likely, she'll bring up the subject again before the night is over.

"We're here," Anneli says excitedly.

Though I prefer to be home, her energy is starting to rub off on me. "Where is here?"

She points at a building where a group of people have congregated outside. Above the entrance is a glowing red sign that reads *Red's Bar & Lounge*. Anneli drives around until she spots an available parking space. I feel out of place as we walk towards the entrance. Everyone looks glamorous and I'm so dull. My wardrobe excludes sexy clothes. This outfit is the best I could come up with on such short notice. My white sandals are a bit dirty and outdated. I'm totally out of my element. I'm at least twenty pounds heavier than my high school days, finally giving me a little ass and the breasts I've always coveted, but I still can't fit into any of Anneli's clothes.

As we walk through the crowded bar, Anneli waves at two men sitting at a round table in the distance.

"You didn't tell me Christian would be here."

They've been in a relationship for a little over a year. I've talked to him through video chat a few times if he happened to be around Anneli during our weekly call. Christian could be a male model with his blond hair, dark amber-colored eyes, and tan skin.

"I may have mentioned we would be here tonight, and he invited himself. It is a free country."

"Who is that sitting at the table with him?"

She clears her throat, looking as guilty as a toddler who's just been caught rummaging in the cookie jar. "Just a friend."

"The same friend I told you not to set me up on a blind date with?"

Christian and his friend have a successful pediatric practice together. Most women would jump at the chance to be introduced to a single handsome doctor, but I'm not interested in dating. I have too many goals I need to accomplish and finding love isn't on the list.

"Maybe."

"I told you no dates."

"It's not a date. We're a group of adults hanging out, pinky swear."

"I would like to snap your pinky in half."

"See? You're violent because you need dick in your life."

"I'm not sure who's worse, you or my mom."

"We want the best for you. Loosen up and live a little. I promise it won't hurt. Also, I heard if you don't use it, it'll shrivel up and fall off. Now smile and put on your best sultry look."

Christian comes around the table, enveloping me in a tight hug and kissing my cheek. "Cin, it's so nice to finally see you in person."

"Likewise."

"This is my friend, Adrian."

Adrian stands, holding out his hand. "It's nice to meet you."

He's sex on a stick—tall and muscular with piercing gray eyes. His shoulder-length jet-black hair is tied at the nape of his neck. I'm hyperaware I resemble a bum. I'm going to kill Anneli. I would've searched for something more appealing to wear had she fessed up about her plan.

"It's nice to meet you too, Adrian."

I sit in the chair he pulls out for me.

"What can I get for you ladies?"

"I'll have a Long Island iced tea," I answer.

"Blue Motorcycle for me." Anneli hated alcohol in high school, but the taste grew on her.

"I'll be right back."

"Isn't he handsome?" Anneli gushes.

"That's beside the point. You tricked me."

"It's not all her fault," Christian chimes in. "Adrian has asked about you constantly ever since seeing a picture of you and Anneli at a track meet together. He really wanted an introduction, so I told him you'd be here tonight."

"Orders up," Adrian announces, placing our drinks on the table.

"Thank you. That was quick," I say.

"The bartender is a friend of mine."

"Christian, I need to talk to you in private about the thing," Anneli says.

"What thing?" he asks, confused.

I narrow my eyes at her, knowing exactly what she's about. I pinch her leg underneath the table, but she grasps my wrist and forces my hand away before dragging Christian from the table.

Fucking asshole.

"Are you enjoying Florida so far?" Adrian asks.

"I've only been here for about twenty-four hours."

"Right." He chuckles.

"I'm sure I'll love it. I needed a change of scenery."

"Whenever you're ready to do some sightseeing, I'll be your personal tour guide."

"I just might take you up on your offer."

"I'm counting on it." His intense eyes roam over my face, like he wants to gobble me up.

"Have you always lived here?" I ask to break the tension.

"Born and raised."

"Where did you go to medical school?"

"Johns Hopkins."

"Why come back?"

"To be near family and accomplish my goal of opening a practice in the community where I grew up."

"Have you always wanted to be a pediatrician?"

"No. I didn't decide on a field of study until high school."

"What prompted your decision?"

"I met some really cool underprivileged kids while mentoring at a Big Brothers program. I developed a strong bond with them and their families. That's how I learned they were not receiving quality medical care. Christian and I never turn anyone away because of their inability to pay."

"You're a bit of a philanthropist."

"It's no big deal."

"Yeah, it is. What you and Christian are doing is amazing."

"Thanks."

"Is that a blush I see?" I tease.

"Maybe." He smiles.

"What activities are you into?"

"Volunteerism, I spend most Saturday mornings at a nonprofit organization where children are taught to swim for free. You should bring your son one day. Anneli told me a little about him."

"Sebastian isn't a strong swimmer, so he could use help honing his skills."

"How old is he?"

"Seven."

"It's a great program and parents can swim with their children."

"Awesome."

I'm happy I came out tonight after all, but still, I'll wait awhile before taking him up on his offer.

ART

I glance around the large banquet hall, located inside the Falcon, at the wealthy and privileged as they socialize. I'm bored out of my fucking mind. It doesn't hurt to show my face, since these bastards fatten my pockets. I'm attending a birthday party for the granddaughter of my grandfather's friend. He continuously tries to play matchmaker the way he did with my father, but I'm never relinquishing my bachelor status. Marriage doesn't benefit me. Sure, I fucked her. She's a prime piece of ass, so of course I accepted her invitation for one night of sex. I have bitches lining up for the chance to fuck me. I'm definitely getting my dick sucked tonight.

Josh sits at the table beside me. "I know what you're thinking."

"What's that?"

"You're wondering which one of these sexy-ass women will be sucking your stick tonight."

"That's not hard to figure out. And stick?"

"You know what I mean."

"I have a dick, not a stick. Compare your own dick to a scrawny stick."

"Not all sticks are skinny. In fact, some are thick and long."

"Shouldn't you be out there sniffing out your next piece of ass?"

"I already found her." He nods towards a redhead.

"Not bad."

"She's a singer."

"I bet you'll have her hitting high notes all night long."

"You know it. Who are you taking home?"

"I haven't chosen yet."

I never fuck any of the women I meet at the hotels. I've made that mistake before. Females are emotional, and I prefer my conquests to not make a scene for employees to gossip about when it's time for them to go. They know all about my reputation. I don't hide who I am. Women often have the misconception they can change me, but after fucking once, I lose interest. I don't take my casual fucks to my mansion either. That's my private sanctuary. I have an oceanfront penthouse in

Brevard County specifically for my pleasure. I moved to Florida about two years ago to open this location. I fell in love with the state, so I chose to make it my permanent residence.

"Trouble imminent."

I glance over and see the birthday girl approaching. Damn, I was hoping she'd be too busy with her friends to pay attention to me.

"Hi, Art."

"Happy Birthday, Ava."

"Thank you. Did you buy me a gift?"

"No."

Women expecting romance from me are in for a rude awakening. I'm incapable of offering them anything, except one night of dick. The one person I gave my heart to betrayed me. It still hurts like it was yesterday. After leaving North Carolina, I spiraled into a black abyss—instigating fights, drinking, using cocaine, and cutting again. Then my brother was born, becoming my salvation. I wanted to do better for him, so I went to rehab and got my shit together. Mason is five now. He looks just like our mother with his strawberry-blond curls and hazel eyes. I have no idea where I would be if it weren't for him. Revenge against Cin receded to the back of my mind.

"Are you up for a rendezvous later?"

"No."

"Okay, maybe next time."

"Not likely."

Tears pool in her eyes before she flees.

"Damn, man. That's cold." Josh laughs.

"Ava knew what she was getting into."

"It's her birthday. You could've made an exception just once in your controlled life."

"My rules are in place for a reason."

"You created the rules, which means you can break them."

"Your redhead is talking to another man. You better go stake your claim or you won't be getting any of her fire crotch tonight."

"I'll talk to you later." He rushes from the table.

Josh has been in Florida for the last three weeks for "cousin bonding" as he calls it. I hope he goes back to Vegas soon. He's a real pain in the ass. Since Josh's dream of football stardom was crushed due to his leg break, he chose to join the family business. Ricky was pissed since he assumed Josh would work with him on the sweet potato farm, but he refused. To ensure the successful expansion of the hotel chain, Josh and I decided to let go of the past. Besides, Cin is to blame for the events that transpired. I'm in charge of the Falcon hotels on the East Coast while Josh takes the lead on the West Coast. A few years ago, we opened the first international location in Paris. Since then, we've launched locations in Sydney, Rome, Dubai, and a few other places—boosting us to billionaire status. The old man oversees those operations. Some hotels are franchised, but we own most of them.

My eyes scan over tonight's pickings when the old man steps into my line of vision. He arrived in Orlando yesterday morning to make an appearance at the party. Thank God he's going to Boston tomorrow evening. I can only handle him in small doses before I go the fuck off.

"Arthur, what did you say to Ava? She's in the restroom with her mother, crying her eyes out."

"I declined her invitation to fuck again. She'll get over it."

"She's a sweet girl. You should give her a real chance."

"If you think she's so sweet, then you fuck her."

"How dare you?" he sputters.

"Oh, I dare that and so much more." I flash my teeth at him. "Get out of my way. I'm searching for my next fuck."

He stomps away.

The ring tone I assigned to Mason blasts from my cell phone.

"What's going on, munchkin?"

"When are you coming home?"

I have sole physical and legal custody of my brother. My father died from a second stroke when Mason was two, liberating my mother from monthly allowances and leaving her a millionaire. She left Mason on my doorstep and moved abroad, which is fine by me, but I hate to see my little brother hurt. The older he gets, the more he asks about her. Mason has questions about his father too, but she hasn't disclosed who he is.

"Not until tomorrow."

"You promised to play video games with me."

"How about I give Ruby tomorrow off and we spend the entire day together?"

"Promise?"

"Scout's honor. Happy now?"

"Yes!"

"Good. See you tomorrow."

"Okay."

I peer towards the crowd again, determined to choose a woman and leave within the next thirty minutes.

Cin

It's been two weeks since I started my position, and everything has been great. A few students were unruly, so the first couple days were a bit rough until it was made clear I'm not a pushover. I spend a quarter of each period teaching health in a classroom. The rest of the time is spent in the gym. My fellow teachers are friendly and helpful. Sebastian likes his new school and has made some friends. My mom walks him to the bus stop every morning and meets him there in the afternoons. Adrian and I have been on several dates. He's simply amazing and has all the qualities I expect in a man, but I prefer to take things slow, which he's agreed to. We're meeting tomorrow morning for Sebastian's first swim lesson.

Anneli called me insane for staying after school on a Friday to grade papers and work on lesson plans. I glance at the clock hanging above the doorway. It's nearly nine. I didn't realize how late it was. I power off the laptop and gather my belongings before heading to the exit. Shit, it's raining hard and I don't have an umbrella. Even if I did, it probably wouldn't do me any good in this heavy downpour. I'll need to be extra cautious driving home. I race across the parking lot towards my car, getting drenched in seconds. Switching on the windshield wipers provides little help.

Twenty minutes later, my car begins to shake and sputter.

"No, no, no, please don't do this to me."

The piece of junk dies in the middle of the fucking exit ramp. I have no money for a tow truck, let alone repairs.

"Piece of fucking shit." I punch the steering wheel.

I rummage through my bag in search of my cell phone. I can't call Anneli. She's working a twelve-hour shift tonight. Where is my cell phone? I dump the contents of my bag on the passenger seat when I fail to find the damn thing. It's not here. Damn, I forgot to get it from the desk drawer.

Fuck!

I'm up shit creek without a damn paddle.

Calm down. Freaking out is not going to help the situation.

Being stranded on an exit ramp on a dark rainy night isn't safe. Any motorist coming around the bend could hit my car, and I might be responsible for the accident. I turn on the emergency lights, then leave the car and walk up the ramp to flag down the next motorist who takes this exit. I'll probably be sick as a dog by tomorrow for standing in the rain. It's going to be a long night.

ART

I'm driving down the highway in my Aston Martin while Carrie—or is her name Cassie? I'll just call her Brunette—slobs all over my dick. She's definitely not a pro, but she's getting the job done. When I turn on the exit ramp, a person appears out of nowhere, wildly flailing their arms.

"Fuck!" I jerk the wheel, crashing into the guardrail.

Brunette sits up, rubbing her face. "What happened?"

"Stay here." I put my dick in my pants before leaving the car in a rage.

"Are you okay?" the stranger asks. "If you weren't a woman, I'd beat the shit out of you!" I shout.

"Fuck you, asshole! You would've seen me if you had been paying attention."

I can barely hear her through the torrential rain, and the headlights from my car reflecting off the pavement make visibility nonexistent.

"What the fuck are you doing out here?"

"It's such a lovely fucking night I decided to take a stroll on the highway!"

"Stupid bitch!"

"My car broke down in the middle of the ramp, jackass! I was trying to prevent an accident!"

"A lot of help you did!"

"Look, can you please help me move my car?"

I want to tell her to fuck off, but it's too dangerous to leave her vehicle where it is. "Get in the damn car," I growl.

"You won't be able to push it by yourself."

Does she think I'm some weakling? "Dammit, woman! Get in the fucking car and turn the wheel right!"

"Bastard!" she shouts, stomping off.

Once the car is safely on the shoulder, I walk towards my own with no intention of saying another word to the woman.

"Wait!"

"What?" I glare at her.

"Would you mind giving me a ride?"

"Yeah, I most certainly would."

"Please. I've been waiting in the rain for almost an hour."

"Didn't you call for a tow truck?"

"I left my cell phone at work."

"You can use mine."

"I can't afford to pay for it."

"Cry me a fucking river. I don't care what the hell you do. Call a taxi, whatever, but I'm not giving you a ride nor am I covering the cost to get your car to a repair shop."

If I ever meet a woman who doesn't have her hand out I'll donate my fortune to charity.

"I didn't ask you to. I'll call a taxi," she snaps.

I let out a frustrated sigh. "Come on. I don't have all damn night."

She follows me to my car and gets into the back. Before I can fully sit my ass in the driver's seat, Brunette complains.

"Who's this? You had me waiting forever."

I've been gone for maybe fifteen minutes. I guess for her that equals forever. I'm about ready to throw both of these bitches out into the storm. My one-night stands are only allowed to open their mouths to partake of my dick or talk nasty shit to me while fucking.

"Shut up. Speak again without permission and I'll take off my sock and stuff it down your damn throat."

My eyes connect with the woman in the back seat through the rearview mirror. Instant recognition renders me paralyzed. I'm taken to the night she ripped my heart in two and shattered my fucking soul. The painful memory dissipates and is replaced with seething rage. Her image has haunted me for so fucking long, but she's finally within my grasp. The thought of making her hurt and beg for mercy fills me with unimaginable pleasure. Damn, my dick is harder than granite. My hands tremble as I salivate with the need to fuck her until my dick is imprinted in the depths of her pussy. I swear if there wasn't a witness here—

She gasps, eyes widening in alarm when she recognizes who I am.

"Cin."

"Art," she croaks.

It's time for her to suffer.

"Where do you live?"

"Why?"

"I'll take you home."

"That won't be necessary. A taxi will do."

"I insist."

"No."

"The only way you're getting home tonight is if it I take you there."

"Baby, let her call for a taxi so we can have some fun," Brunette says, gripping my thigh.

I push her hand away. "I told you to shut up." I glance at Cin. "Address."

I click on the child safety locks when she reaches for the door handle.

"This is kidnapping."

"I'm just being a good citizen."

"I'd rather sit here all night than give you my address."

I see the fire in her hasn't been extinguished, but she won't win this round of the Art and Cin game show. I grab my cell phone, scroll through the contacts, then click on Logan's name. He answers after the first ring. I pay him top dollar to do my biddings at the drop of a dime.

"What can I do for you?"

"I need an address for a Cinnamon Belo. You have fifteen minutes."

"You got it."

"You're invading my privacy," she snaps.

"Amazing what money can buy, isn't it?"

I receive a text with her address in less than ten minutes.

"Good, you live close." I start the engine and leave the ramp.

"What are you waiting for?" I ask Brunette.

"What do you mean?"

"Finish sucking my dick."

"What?"

"I don't repeat myself, ever."

After a few seconds of indecision, she gives in. The bimbo doesn't want to upset her potential meal ticket. She pulls my thick length out and starts going to town like a good little whore.

"Let me out of this car right now!" Cin yells.

I overexaggerate my groans to piss her off further. "Just like that, baby. Suck the skin off my dick."

"You're depraved!"

"This is the best head I've ever had."

"I hope you rot in hell!"

"Do you mind? This is a beautiful moment and you're ruining it."

Man, that comment sets her the fuck off. Her body shakes in anger as she shouts obscenities at the top of her lungs. I rapidly guide Brunette's head up and down while watching Cin in the mirror. I hate her with a passion, but I want to fuck her senseless. I groan, releasing my semen down Brunette's throat.

She sits up with a satisfied expression on her face. "I have a lot more tricks to show you, baby."

I bring my vehicle to a sudden stop on the shoulder, then roughly grab Cin's hair before switching off the locks.

"Let me go!" She claws at me.

I glance at Brunette. "Get out."

"Excuse me?"

"You served your purpose."

"Is this a joke?"

"Am I laughing?"

"You can't leave me stranded here."

I pull a hundred-dollar bill from my wallet and toss it at her while maintaining my hold on a struggling Cin. "I lied about your dick-sucking abilities. You should practice a little more. On a scale from one to ten, I'll give you a four."

"Fucking asshole! I'll tell everyone what a lunatic you are!"

"Sweetheart, they already know."

She exits the car and slams the door shut behind her. I enable the child locks once more, ensuring Cin can't escape.

"How can you be so cruel?"

"Easy."

"You're still the same bastard after all these years."

"I'm far from the same. I've evolved into super-bastard."

"How wonderful," she says sarcastically.

"Relax, she's a resilient whore like you. I'm sure she'll figure something out."

"I want out of this car!"

"Yeah, well, I didn't want you to stab me in the back."

"I never said a thing to anyone!"

"How did the old man and Ricky find out?"

"I have no idea, but it wasn't from me!"

"You're a whore and a liar."

"I could care less what you believe."

"Climb up here."

"Fuck you."

Thank God. I was hoping for her defiance. "I kind of figured you'd say that."

I seize her hair and forcibly haul her over the console. She falls to the floorboard with her ass sticking up right beside my face. I use the opportunity to bury my nose between her butt cheeks.

"You goddamn creep! This is sexual assault!" she yells, kicking her legs wildly.

"I'm just taking a whiff. Sweaty ass that's been marinating all day smells the best."

I help her into the passenger seat, then deliver a hard whack to her leg.

"Did you just pop my leg like I'm a disobedient child?"

"Disobeying me results in swift discipline."

I maneuver back onto the highway, intent on getting to our destination. My dick will be inside her tonight—raw, so I can feel every inch of her cunt. Fuck,

I'm still weak for her. All the feelings I thought had disappeared long ago came flooding back with a vengeance. That's how much of an impact she has on me. She flayed me open, cutting deeper than the razor I used to tear open my flesh. I'll have my revenge while enjoying her body—her very delectable body. Her wet T-shirt and basketball shorts mold to her amazing form. She's gained a little weight, filling her out in all the right places. The girl she was doesn't compare to the woman she's become. She's fucking beautiful. Her long braid still falls to her hip bone, minus the pink tips. I'll figure out a way to keep her close and hurt her.

"When did you move here? Do you live alone?"

She could have a boyfriend, but that didn't deter me then and it sure as hell isn't going to stop me now. If she's in a relationship, I'm breaking that shit up pronto. Sharing her again is not an option.

"None of your damn business."

I deliver a bruising slap to her leg.

"Stop hitting me!" she demands.

"Then be a good little girl and answer my fucking questions."

"Kiss my ass."

Another hit cracks across her soft skin.

"Stop! You're hurting me!"

"It's supposed to hurt."

I raise my hand, prepared to strike, but she quickly responds. "I moved to Florida a little over a month ago."

I glance at her left finger. "No husband or perhaps you took off your wedding ring to cheat tonight. That's something you're very familiar with."

She stubbornly clenches her jaw.

"Boyfriend?"

She presses her lips together in a firm line.

"Do you want to get hit again?"

"If you lay one more finger on me, I'm going to go apeshit on you."

"Don't test my savage," I say menacingly.

"No boyfriend," she grits out.

"See, that wasn't so hard. Do you live alone?"

"No."

"Roommate?"

"My mom."

"That's it?" I dig my nails into her thigh when she doesn't answer. "I asked is that it?"

She grasps my wrist, attempting to pry my hand off her. "Yes!"

"Don't overcomplicate things. Whatever doesn't come easy for me is taken by force."

I turn left into a parking lot. I survey the area. "You live here?"

"Yeah."

"It's a dump."

"It's what I can afford. Thanks for the ride."

"Aren't you going to invite me in for a drink?"

"No."

"I insist."

"Tough shit."

"I'm coming inside whether you like it or not."

"Fine."

"I'm glad we understand each other."

"Fuck you!" Cin yells, bolting from the car.

I immediately give chase. My heart rate increases, sending adrenaline coursing through my veins. I'm hot on her heels as she makes it inside the building. The thrill of the hunt is intoxicating. Cin bursts into a stairwell, racing up the steps two at a time. She flings open a door and darts into a hallway but doesn't get far before I tackle her. I'm so hungry for her I'll fuck her anywhere, even on this disgusting floor.

"I like it when you run," I murmur in her ear.

"You could be seen assaulting me at any moment."

"Am I supposed to be scared?" I say, flipping her over and settling between her legs.

"I'll scream."

"Go ahead." I kiss along her jawline.

I miss and hate her so fucking much. She vehemently thrashes beneath me, but she's no match for my strength. My wandering hand admires her lovely curves, then pushes under the waistband of her shorts. Sharp nails rake across my face.

"Goddamn it," I growl, pinning her wrists above her head to prevent further attack.

Her big doe eyes widen in fear of retaliation. I touch the torn flesh using my free hand, before smearing the blood coating my fingertips over her plump lips. I venture into her shorts for a second time.

"Remember, you drew first blood." I sink my teeth into her shoulder hard enough to break skin. She lets out a loud scream that ends on a whimper as my finger massages her clit.

A door opens to the left of us. "What's going on out here?" an elderly man asks.

"Mind your business," I snap.

"Don't you young people have common decency anymore?"

"Get back in your apartment, old-timer, before you get hurt," I growl.

"I'm calling the police." He slams the door.

"Nosy motherfucker." I stand, dragging Cin with me. "We'll finish this in your apartment."

"No, we're not."

I latch onto the back of her neck, forcing her forward. "Yes, the fuck we are."

Cin swings around unexpectedly, using the element of surprise to punch me in the nose and knee me in the dick. She jets down the hallway.

I recover after a few seconds, but it's too late, she made it inside the safety of her apartment. "Run away, little birdie, I'll catch you soon enough."

I hurry from the building, not wanting to bump into the police. Once inside my car, I call Logan.

"What can I do for you?"

"I want to know everything about Cinnamon Belo. Dig so deep she gets a fucking nosebleed."

"You got it."

"Have the report first thing in the morning."

"Will do."

I'll do whatever it takes to get her back in my bed, no matter the cost. I'd sell my soul to the devil if I had one.

Cin

I look through the peephole, heart pounding in my chest, praying he doesn't kick the door in, waking up my mom and Sebastian in the process. I breathe a sigh of relief when he doesn't come knocking. Relocating here was supposed to be a new beginning. I didn't expect to collide with the past. If it were possible to reason with him, we could've had a civil conversation. He has it stuck in his mind that I sold him out. This isn't the last I've seen of him. I walk into the living room on shaky legs and drop onto the sofa.

Art no longer sports hoop earrings—or a nose or lip ring for that matter. He's all man now, his body definitely harder and more muscular. He must have a rigid exercise routine. I thought a few of my ribs would be cracked from his tackle. Add in his classic good looks, mesmerizing green eyes, and glossy black hair, and he's a woman's fantasy on the surface. But a monster lurks underneath. He threw that woman out into the storm with no remorse after she gave him a blowjob!

I'll ask Anneli if I can borrow money for a tow truck. I'm such a fucking leech. Just when things were going great, the universe bent me over to fuck me in the ass with no lube. I quietly go into the den to grab my mom's cell phone to call Anneli. I'm not sure what time it is. She could still be at work or just getting home.

"Hi, Missy."

"It's me."

"Why are you calling me from your mom's phone?"

"I left mine at work."

"What's up? You're usually asleep at this time, old woman."

"You're a jackass."

"Well someone needs to get fucked ASAP. When are you going to stop being a prude and fuck Adrian?"

"Do you have an off switch?"

"Nope."

"You're a complete mess." I laugh.

"I can't help it. I was born this way," she says cheekily.

"Are you home yet?"

"Yep, I just got in."

"I've had a hell of a night."

"Give me all the details."

"My car broke down in the middle of an exit ramp on the way home."

"Damn."

"You haven't heard the worst of it."

"Well, don't keep me in suspense."

"Guess who came to my rescue but definitely wasn't a knight in shining armor?"

"Tell me already!"

"Art."

"No fucking way."

"I almost pissed my pants. It was raining so hard, I didn't recognize him until I got in his car."

Anneli stays quiet as I tell her every single detail of tonight's events.

"Wow, just, wow. Do you think he'll come back?"

"Definitely."

"What are you going to do if he does?"

"I can't let him fuck up my life."

"We'll destroy him if he tries."

It'll take a battalion to defeat him.

"What are you going to do about your car?"

"I was wondering if you could lend me the money for a tow truck. I'll pay it back in a couple weeks, I swear."

"Of course. I know a good mechanic. He's affordable and won't cheat you."

"You're too good to me."

"That's what friends are for."

"Okay," I say, yawning. "I'm going to shower, then head to bed."

"Talk to you later."

Art is going to come at me from all angles. I need to prepare myself.

Cin

"Thank you for taking me to get my cell phone. It wasn't exactly on the way to where we're going."

"Honestly, it's no problem at all." Adrian squeezes my left hand.

"Are we there yet?" Sebastian asks from the back seat.

"Have a little patience, kiddo," I say.

"But it's taking forever!"

"We'll be there in about ten minutes." Adrian chuckles.

"Sorry about that."

"Hey, I'm used to being around impatient children. I can handle it, no sweat."

I was nervous about Adrian and Sebastian meeting, but they hit it off. He's the first man I've ever introduced to Sebastian. My mom would not stop telling him how handsome he is and talked about my attributes nonstop, even mentioning how I'm ready to settle down and have more babies. Needless to say, I made sure we left in a hurry. That woman sure knows how to embarrass me.

"Wow!" I exclaim when Adrian pulls into the parking lot of a huge two-level building with a flawless manicured lawn.

"We're here! We're here!" Sebastian yells in excitement.

Kids That Swim adorns the front in colorful letters.

"There are three outdoor and three indoor pools. The outdoor pools are usually closed after a heavy rain to prevent any injuries since the ground is wet. Beginner, intermediate, and advanced swim lessons are offered every two hours. The rest of the time, it's free swim. Since Sebastian isn't a beginner, I think he could be put with the intermediate-level swimmers. There's also an arcade, a small library, and a break room with vending machines.

"Mom, I want to play games in the arcade."

"We can after the swim lesson."

"Yay!"

"The president's office, human resources, and payroll are located on the second floor."

"Paid positions are available?"

"Yes. Interested in applying?"

"I could use a second income."

"Go for it. You can complete an application before we leave."

Sebastian darts from the car the moment Adrian pulls into a vacant spot. He jumps up and down as he waits for us.

"Man, kids are quick."

"Except when they're asked to clean up," I joke.

We follow a skipping Sebastian into the building. Life-sized Marvel characters are stationed throughout the lobby and painted on the walls too. A spacious sitting area is to the right of the reception desk, and a spiral staircase is to the left.

"This place is so cool," Sebastian says in awe.

"Good morning, Madelyn." Adrian greets a woman sitting behind the front desk.

"Good morning."

"This is Cinnamon and her amazing son, Sebastian, who's here to become a stronger swimmer."

"Excellent, it's nice to meet you and your cutie pie."

"Boys can't be called cutie pie!"

"Oh my. I'm so sorry. What on earth was I thinking calling a big strapping boy like you 'cutie pie'? Will you forgive me?"

"Well okay, but just this once."

"Thank you so much." Madelyn winks at me. "Tragedy averted."

"That was a close call." I laugh.

"I just need for you to complete some paperwork." She hands me a thick packet and pen.

"Cin."

Is my mind playing tricks on me? Please tell me that's not who I think it is calling my name. I slowly turn my head to see Art descending the stairs with a little boy at his side. I wonder if that's his son. Art is too damn sexy for his own good in a pair of dark tan slacks with a white short-sleeved shirt displaying his fire tattoo.

"What a pleasant surprise, Art. It's been a while since I bumped into you here." Adrian shakes hands with my tormentor. "I see you two have already met."

"Yeah, we go way back," Art says.

"What a coincidence. Cin and I have been dating for about six weeks."

The vein in Art's neck beats wildly, contradicting his calm demeanor.

"Make sure you keep an eye on this one. She had all the boys running after her in high school."

I'm sweating bullets, scared to death of what he'll tell Adrian about me.

"I can handle it." He turns to me. "Art started this nonprofit in honor of his brother."

Art smiles—if you could call the expression he's making a smile.

I can't form words. My cognitive function is disappearing. There's the universe fucking with me again.

"Are you okay?" Adrian asks.

I can only nod my head in response.

"I'm bored," Sebastian complains.

"Mason, why don't you take Sebastian to the arcade? Is that okay with you, Cinnamon? Just until you finish the paperwork. Children can get restless so quickly," Madelyn suggests.

"That's fine." I lick my dry lips.

Both boys run off.

"Where did you two meet?"

"Senior year in high school," Art answers.

My body begins to shiver under his piercing glare.

"Cin is interested in a position here." Adrian is oblivious to the tension surrounding us.

"I'll interview you today."

"No, that's okay. I'm sure you're really busy."

"I am, but I can make time for an old friend."

"I can't stay out late today. I have to get home and help my mom do something." Fuck, I couldn't think of anything else to say.

"It'll only take twenty minutes, tops."

"I'm not dressed appropriately, and I don't have my resume."

"Cin, you shouldn't pass up this opportunity," Adrian chimes in.

"Your outfit won't be a problem and you can email your resume later," Art says.

"Okay," I agree reluctantly. "Thank you."

"You're welcome. Since you've been such a good friend, I'm glad to rearrange my schedule just for you."

I'll work for you when hell freezes over, asshole. I'll come clean to Adrian about my past with Art before he fills his head with lies.

ART

I walk the perimeter of the pool under the guise of watching Mason swim, but my attention is really on Cin. She effortlessly propels herself across the surface of the water. As she swims, the tattoo on the back of her left shoulder mocks me. It signifies my exoneration from my own personal hell, but the freedom I achieved was only a camouflage, releasing me into a bigger birdcage. I want to cut it from her flesh. I nearly lost my damn mind after catching a glimpse of her bikini-clad body when she left the changing room. Everything about her is fucking perfect, from her small delicate feet to her slightly rounded hips, juicy tits, firm thighs, and soft ass.

It took every ounce of my willpower not to throw her to the floor and fuck her like a savage caveman. I would've laid the world at her feet had she not betrayed me. My dick twitches as I imagine pushing into her tight heat. I never wanted to fuck a woman so badly in my life. I head to my office to wait for her. There's no doubt in my mind I'll be riding Cin hard tonight.

Cin

My frayed nerves are stretched taut as I stand in front of Art's office door.

You can do this. Go in there and tell him to fuck off.

I count to twenty, steeling myself before knocking.

"Come in."

I enter hell to find the devil sitting behind a large wooden desk.

"I was wondering how long you planned to stand out there."

Art's roaming eyes make me feel exposed though I have on my standard baggy shorts and T-shirt.

"I was hoping you'd keep on your bikini for the interview." He motions his hand towards a chair. "Please have a seat."

"Cut the shit. You know damn well I would never work for you." I close the door but stay where I am.

"Sit the fuck down."

"No. Tell me what your angle is," I demand.

"Does your boyfriend know you're a backstabbing slut?"

"I own cheating on Trevor with you, but I never exposed your secret to anyone!" I'm tired of sounding like a broken record.

"I should rip your lying tongue from your fucking mouth," he says angrily.

"Try it and I'll bite your fingers off."

He opens a drawer and tosses a manila folder on the desk. "This is your life."

"You had a background check done on me?"

"I did."

"For what purpose?"

"Leverage to get what I want."

"Which is?"

"Sex."

"But you hate me."

"My mind knows that, but my dick just wants to fuck."

"That'll never happen."

"You wanna bet?"

"I have better things to do than have a pointless conversation with you." I turn to leave.

"I'll pay you half a million dollars for unlimited access to your pussy for six months."

I face him again. "What type of bullshit are you trying to feed me?"

"I have your attention now, I see." He smirks.

"Take your money, and stick it right up your ass."

"You're struggling to make ends meet every single month. Soon you'll have to start making payments on your student loans, not to mention you no longer have transportation."

"My car will be repaired."

"Your engine is shot. Do you have the funds to replace it?"

"How do you know? The mechanic hasn't called with a diagnostic yet."

"I made it my business to know every minuscule detail of your life. Trevor is Sebastian's father but wants nothing to do with him and hasn't provided a dime towards his upbringing. You rarely hear from your father since he remarried. Your mother doesn't work due to the injury she sustained from the boot. How does it feel to be the cause of your mother's blindness and the reason she suffers from debilitating migraines?"

Tears roll down my cheeks.

"Crying won't undo the damage you've caused."

"You don't understand how much that night has tormented me."

"Do right by Sebastian and your mother and take the offer. It's more than you deserve."

I could wipe my debt clean and have thousands left to spare.

"I want the money up front."

"You will receive the money after the six months is over, not a day before."

"I can't trust you."

"I'll keep my end of the agreement. You have my word."

"That's not good enough."

"It's all you're getting."

"Give me a contract and we have a deal."

"It's a verbal agreement or nothing at all."

"That's not fair."

"Life isn't fair. But I'll sweeten the pot by paying for your mother's medical expenses starting now."

Do I really want to make a deal with the devil?

He glances at the watch donning his wrist. "Sixty seconds."

"Sixty seconds until what?"

"Until the offer expires."

The damn bastard has me exactly where he wants me.

"I agree."

"Jump."

"Excuse me?" I ask, confused.

He shakes his head. "Wrong fucking response. When I tell you to do something, you fucking do it, no questions. Do I make myself clear?"

"Yes," I bite out.

"Get on your hands and knees."

My mind rebels against obeying his command. He watches me with a hawk-like gaze, waiting to see if I'll follow his order. I slowly descend to the floor.

"Crawl to me."

He's treating me like a fucking dog.

"I want zero fucking hesitation when I give an order. Get the fuck over here!" he bellows.

I crawl across the floor, coming to a stop in front of him.

He unzips his pants, freeing his length. "Apologize."

"Huh?"

"Apologize to my dick for kneeing him yesterday."

"No way."

He slaps his hardness against my forehead. "The sooner you learn to obey, the easier it'll be for you."

"Do that again and I'll bite it off."

"I dare you, little birdie. But understand the moment I feel your teeth I'm going to tie you to this fucking chair and use pliers to pull each one out." Art points to his dick. "He's waiting."

"I'm sorry," I grit out.

"Tsk, tsk, tsk, say it like you mean it."

Ugh! Fucking asshole!

"I'm sorry," I say, sweetly.

"For what?"

"Kneeing you."

"And?"

"It'll never happen again."

 "Good, now I want my dick touching your tonsils."

Art twists his hands in my hair and rams his dick down my throat, viciously fucking my mouth. Saliva drips down my chin as I gag. I brace my hands on his thighs, attempting to break away.

"It's more fun when you struggle."

 He holds my head in place, grinding his hips against my face harder. I'm on the verge of emptying the contents of my stomach when his salty cum fills my mouth.

"Fuck," he groans, pulling his semi-hard dick from my mouth.

"You almost suffocated me!" I yell.

"I'll give you a two on a scale from one to ten. At least Brunette was a four."

"You're sadistic."

"I know, and it's fucking fantastic." He points at the semen soaking into the carpet. "You spilled some."

"So."

"Lick it up."

"What?"

"You can't leave the table until you've eaten all your food." He leans close to my face. "Finish your meal."

"No."

He leaves the chair in a flash, gripping the back of my neck and pushing my face into the carpet.

"Lick it the fuck up," he growls in my ear.

I whimper as he applies more pressure, but still I refuse.

"You won't win this battle, little birdie."

He twists my arm up my back as he maneuvers behind me, forcing me to my knees. He jerks my shorts and bikini bottoms down.

"It's going to bring me so much joy breaking you."

"What are you doing?" I ask, whimpering.

He positions his erection at the entrance of my ass. "I'm sure being fucked in the ass with no lube hurts like a motherfucker."

He thrusts forward. The searing pain is unbearable.

"Art, no! It hurts so bad!"

"And that's only the tip. Imagine how painful it'll be if I penetrated you fully. Do you want me to make you bleed?"

"No!"

"Then. Lick. The. Carpet." He emphasizes each word.

My tongue darts out, licking up his essence.

"This is going to be a long six months if you continue to fight me." He releases me and moves back to his chair.

"You could've broken my arm." I glare at him while rubbing my sore limb.

"Fix your clothes and have a seat. I need to go over the rules with you."

I drop down into the chair with more force than necessary.

"Rule one: No sharing you this time. Break it off with Adrian the moment you leave this office."

"He brought me here. How will I get home?"

"I'll call a taxi."

"I can do it later, not here."

"Do it now!" he shouts.

"Fine."

"Rule two: You're not allowed to talk, smile, or even look at another man."

"That's ridiculous! I have male colleagues."

"You better figure something out because if you break any of my rules, heads are going to roll. Understand?"

"Yes," I grit out.

"Rule three: Obey me without question."

"Is that it, or do you want my soul too?"

"I already own it."

"Fucking asshole," I grumble under my breath.

"What's that?"

"Nothing."

"Be at my place by eight tonight. Tardiness is not acceptable, so make sure you're on time."

I salute him. "Sir, yes, sir!"

"Now you're getting it." He blows me a kiss. "I'll text you the address."

"Of course you know my cell phone number," I say sarcastically.

He laughs. "You can go now."

I storm out of his office, dreading what I have to do next.

Cin

"Did something happen between you and Adrian?" Mom asks, turning her attention from the television.

We've been parked on the sofa for the last hour watching our favorite sitcom while Sebastian plays on the floor with his toys.

"No, everything is good."

I feel like the scum of the earth for not being honest with her, but I'm not ready to have this conversation.

"You seem out of sorts since getting home."

"I'm fine. I promise."

"All right," she says, leaning back against the cushions.

My imagination is working overtime, conjuring up all sorts of things Art has planned for me tonight. He probably has a secret dungeon to torture me in. But I'm resolved to face whatever he throws at me head-on. Loud banging sounds at the front door, startling me.

"There's no way you can avoid me now that we live in the same state!" Anneli yells.

Oh, fuck.

"What's going on?" Mom asks.

"Nothing, you know how theatrical Anneli can be."

She raises an eyebrow, giving me a skeptical look. I hurriedly move towards the door when the loud banging starts again. A noise complaint is the last thing I need after living here for less than two months. It's bad enough my neighbor caught me in a compromising position last night. Hopefully he didn't recognize me.

"Hold your horses! I'm coming!" I swing the door open.

"You've been ignoring me!" Anneli yells.

"Shhh."

"Don't you 'shhh' me. And move out of the way so I can come inside." She brushes past me.

"I was going to call you in the morning."

"Oh no, you've got some explaining to do and I want answers now!"

Adrian was livid I abruptly ended our courtship earlier. Soon after, Anneli started texting and calling.

"Hey, Missy." She waves.

"Hi, sweetheart. Are you and Cin having a fight?"

"We most certainly are."

"We're not," I counter.

"Auntie Anneli!" Sebastian runs over to wrap his skinny arms around her torso. "Did you bring a special treat for me?"

"Not this time, kiddo, but next time I'll bring five pounds of candy so you can drive your mom crazy."

I scrunch my face at her. "He'll be staying with you until all the sugar is out of his system."

"Beat it, squirt. I have a bone to pick with your mom." She grabs my arm and pulls me into the bedroom before closing the door for privacy.

Anneli will probably try to persuade me to change my mind, but I won't budge. My mom and Sebastian deserve the finer things in life, and I'll be providing it to them by any means necessary.

"What the hell is going on, Cin? Adrian is pissed, and I don't blame him."

I sit on the bed. "I ran into Art again today."

"What the fuck does that have to do with you and Adrian?"

"Everything."

She sits beside me. "What happened?"

"Art owns the nonprofit organization where Adrian volunteers."

"Did he threaten you? Is that why you ended it?"

"No."

"You blindsided him without explanation! He's a good man, Cin!"

"Art offered me half a million dollars to sleep with him for six months."

"The fuck?" she whispers.

"Do you know what that money could mean for my mom, Sebastian, and me? They're worth more to me than Adrian. We only just started dating and it may not lead anywhere."

"Oh my God. That's a lot of fucking money."

"Exactly. He's going to pay for my mom's medical expenses too. I'd be a fool to pass up an opportunity like this."

"But are you willing to sell your soul for it? You're a fish swimming around in the river, having the time of your life, and he's the fisherman who dangles a big fat juicy worm right before your eyes. The prize is too irresistible to pass up, so you latch on, not realizing you'll be gutted and eaten. Do you have any clue what he's capable of?"

"No, I don't, but my decision is final."

"You need to think about your safety."

"He's just hurt. That's all. I've helped him overcome his pain before."

"Oh my God, stop being so fucking stupid. The big difference is he believes you caused his hurt this time around. He'll destroy you."

"It's a chance I'm willing to take."

"Can I come in?" Mom calls.

"Keep your lips zipped about this in front of my mom. I haven't told her yet."

"I should, so she can talk some sense into you."

"Anneli," I say in exasperation.

"Okay, fine."

"Come in, Mom."

She enters the bedroom carrying three boxes with a huge smile on her face. "These were just delivered for you."

"I didn't order anything," I say, confused.

"There's an envelope with your name on it. I'm sure it's from Adrian," Mom says, delighted.

I take the boxes and place them on the bed beside me before opening the envelope.

The packages contain your required attire for tonight. Wear your hair down. Refusal to follow the instructions provided will result in severe punishments.

Sincerely,

Your Owner, a.k.a. Pussy Connoisseur

P.S. Don't fuck with me.

"What does it say?" Mom asks.

"Nothing important." I stuff the card back in the envelope before sliding it into my pocket.

"Oh, it must be private." Mom winks.

I open the first package and find a pair of black I'm-going-to-break-my-fucking-neck stilettos.

"Oh, those are nice." Mom picks one up for further inspection.

Anneli whistles. "Those are red bottoms."

"What?"

She rolls her eyes. "How can you be so fashion deficient? They're designed by Christian Louboutin and are very expensive."

"Well, I'm going to kill myself in them."

"Don't be so melodramatic. Just walk very, very slowly."

"Gee, thanks for the advice," I say sarcastically.

"You are most welcome, dumpling," Anneli replies sweetly.

Package number two has a barely there, skimpy-as-fuck red lace bra and G-string set. The tiny triangle bottoms will give me little coverage.

"Oh my goodness." Mom fans herself.

"Damn, it looks like you're going to have a lot of fun tonight. I can't wait to see what's behind door number three."

I hesitate to open the last package. Art will probably have me looking like a cheap hooker. I'm pleasantly surprised to discover a simple yet elegant, thigh-length black satin dress with skinny straps.

"It's beautiful," I say.

"What time is your date?" Mom asks.

"I'm supposed to be there at eight."

"But it's almost seven o'clock. Shouldn't you shower and get dressed?" Anneli asks.

"Oh shit." I flee to the bathroom.

This is so not good.

Cin

The driver stops in front of the luxury building twenty minutes past the time I was directed to arrive. I nearly fall out of the car in my hurry to get inside. At my approach the doorman greets me with a friendly smile and opens the door.

"Thank you."

"You're welcome. Enjoy your night."

"You do the same."

Surprisingly, Art hasn't called or texted, but I'm not relieved. His silence speaks volumes. There's no telling what kind of evil thoughts are running through his mind this very second. With the killer stilettos in my hands, I make a mad dash pass the concierge desk towards the elevators, barefoot.

"Excuse me," a woman sitting behind the desk calls.

"Yes?"

"You have to show ID and sign in."

"I'm really in a rush. Can you make an exception?"

"I'm sorry, unfortunately that won't be possible. It's policy for nonresidents to show identification and sign in."

I grudgingly walk over and hand her my driver's license before writing my information in the visitor's log.

"Ms. Belo, an access badge for the penthouse elevator has been left for you. It's the last one on the right."

I nod, taking the offered badge. Clutching the death traps and handbag to my chest like a protective shield, I step onto the elevator that'll deliver me to the gates of hell. Goose bumps break out over my flesh when the doors open. Art is nowhere in sight, but I know he's out there, waiting. What will he do to me? The not knowing causes tremors to rack my body.

"What are you waiting for? Come out and play, little birdie." His voice echoes, so it's hard to discern which direction it's coming from.

"I lost track of time."

"Excuses, excuses."

Slowly, I emerge into the dimly lit foyer, glancing around for any sign of danger. Suddenly, my body is flung to the floor. My teeth sink into my tongue on impact, filling my mouth with blood. The stilettos and handbag scatter across the glossy marble.

I attempt to get up, but Art places his foot in the middle of my back, forcing me down.

"Why aren't the shoes on your fucking feet?"

"They're difficult to walk in."

"I don't give a fuck! I instructed you to wear them!" He removes his foot. "Crawl."

Art kicks me in the ass as I move along, causing me to crash to the floor again.

"Bastard," I mumble.

"What the fuck did you call me?" he shouts.

"Bastard!"

He latches onto my hair and drags me into the living room.

"Let me go!" I yell, biting his ankle.

"Fuck!"

He hauls me up and seizes my throat in a brutal hold as I beat on his chest.

"A fighter until the very end, I see."

"Damn right," I choke out.

He slams me against the wall, rattling my brain.

"Give up," he says, squeezing harder.

My arms become weaker, eventually falling to my sides due to lack of oxygen. Blackness dances at the edge of my vision.

"That's right, little birdie. Give up. You'll never be able to beat me, but it's entertaining when you try."

Air fills my starving lungs when he releases my throat.

"I want you naked, now."

Art pulls his belt off when I don't obey. "Try me."

I'm not ready to find out if he would really spank me, so instead of defying him like my instincts demand, I take the dress off. I tremble under his intense gaze. Art's erection is visible through his pants. Next, I unhook my bra and bring the straps down my arms to fall the floor. He reaches out and slides his hand over my skin in feather-light touches before dropping to his knees.

"I'll take these off." He rips the G-string from my body.

"Damn, these are soaked. Does fighting me make you horny?"

It does, but I refuse to admit the truth to him. "No."

He smacks me hard on the ass. "Don't lie."

Standing, he brings the fabric to his nose and inhales deeply.

"I've missed this smell," he groans. "Did you shave for me?" He glides his fingers through my bare pussy.

"No, I did it for Adrian." I smirk.

Another lie, but I needed at least one small victory in the game of cat and mouse we're playing. Art's body begins to shake ever so slightly, and his facial features transform into granite. Fury lurks in the depths of his bright green eyes. He caresses the side of my face with the back of his hand.

"People disappear every day without a trace, never to be found again, little birdie."

Shivers run down my spine at the ominous threat.

"Accidents happen every day too. It would be a shame if something happened to this pretty face. Who would want you then?"

"You don't scare me," I say with false bravado.

"If that were the truth, you wouldn't be shaking." He smirks.

The dangerous aura that surrounded Art in high school has increased tenfold. He is not a man anyone would be stupid enough to cross.

"Put your shoes on. I'll be back."

I eye the monstrosities with contempt as I walk to where they lie on the floor. I pick them up, seriously contemplating throwing them out the fucking window until I remember the belt. It couldn't hurt that badly. In the end, I choose to slip them on my feet. Despite my best efforts to stay completely still, my legs wobble. He returns with a lit cigar in one hand and a glass filled with amber-colored liquor in the other. Art's gaze roams my body as he takes a long puff of his cigar, then slowly releases the smoke from his nostrils and mouth.

He sits on the sofa. "Come over here."

It takes considerable strength and balance not to fall on my ass as I gradually stumble over. I stop directly in front of him.

"On occasion, you will be required to wear heels when you're with me, so it's time for you to practice. Walk back and forth in a straight line."

"And if I break my ankle?"

"Practice will still continue until I say otherwise, so you better hope you don't. You may begin." He sips the dark liquid.

Fuck, I should've thrown these motherfuckers out the damn window. I turn, stumbling across the length of the living room. Shit, this is the most strenuous exercise I've ever done. My left ankle gives out, and I fall hard to the floor.

"The way your ass jiggled at impact was fucking amazing, baby."

"Fuck you," I say, pushing to my feet.

My eyes connect with Art's as I double back. He places the glass on the floor before pulling his dick from his pants and leisurely moving his hand up and down his thick length. My mouth waters at the raw erotic sight. I remember the feel of his manhood deliciously filling and stretching me. I switch directions again, only taking a few steps before being grabbed from behind, one hand clutching my breast while the other grasps my cunt. I moan, biting my bottom lip.

"Do you know what goes perfect with a cigar and whiskey?" He kisses my ear.

I shake my head.

"Pussy."

He throws me roughly to the floor. "Lie on your back and spread your legs."

I roll over, opening myself up for him. My pussy clenches in anticipation as he undresses, then descends to his knees and buries his face between my thighs. He devours my pussy. There's no other word to describe it. My hips gyrate against his mouth as he sucks and flicks his tongue across my clit. I lose myself in the tornado building inside me until finally I reach climax, screaming out in pleasure. Art crawls up my body, capturing my lips in a kiss. No, not a kiss—a branding. Our tongues battle for supremacy as we cling to each other. He lifts my legs over his shoulders before driving his length inside me, stretching my pussy to capacity.

"Oh my God," I whisper as he groans.

He starts fucking me uncontrollably, not giving my body time to adjust to his intrusion.

It's heaven and hell.

"So warm and wet," he growls.

Art relentlessly pummels through my tight hole, stroking deeper with each thrust forward. Our moans along with the sound of flesh hitting flesh creates sensual music. I'm losing my mind to this passion and I don't give a damn. He fucks me with a ferocity that should scare me shitless, but it doesn't. Instead, I dig my nails into his ass, encouraging him.

"You can't come in me. I'm not on birth control."

"Fuck that, I'm not pulling out."

"I'm serious."

"I haven't fucked you in eight years. There's no way in hell I'm pulling out."

As he pumps his hips faster, another orgasm tears through me, causing my pussy to spasm. It's a wonderful torment.

"Cin," Art shouts, reaching his climax. "Fuck you for making me feel this way."

"You could've just left me alone."

"If only I had the fucking willpower, but you have this hold over me. Maybe if you told the truth, I could move on."

"You don't believe the truth."

He stands, violently yanking me up with him. He tugs me across the living room towards the spiral staircase. "I'm not done with you."

I trip several times as he drags me up the stairs. "Slow down!"

He pulls me into a scarcely furnished but huge bedroom with floor-to-ceiling windows overlooking the beach. He leads me to a wooden plank mounted to the wall with straps attached.

"What are you doing?" I struggle vehemently to get away.

"Don't be afraid, little birdie."

The big strong bastard has both my wrists secured to the straps in less than two minutes.

He's going to torture me now.

I'm facing the wall, so I have no idea what's coming next.

Art gets on his knees and slips the stilettos from my feet. Without the added height, only the tips of my toes touch the floor. He stuns me by spreading my butt cheeks and licking the puckered hole found there.

"I remember when my fingers explored back here in high school." He places a kiss on the virgin area. "Have you ever had anal sex?"

"No and I don't want to."

"That's too bad." He stands.

"What does that mean?"

"You're about to find out." He walks away.

"Where are you going?"

Art returns, startling me when he rubs a cool gel between my ass cheeks.

"What is that?"

"Lubricant."

"Please don't!" I shout.

"Don't tense up. It'll be easier for you."

"No!"

He positions his dick at my entrance and begins to penetrate me slowly.

"I'm begging you not to do this!"

"Calm down and take deep breaths." He slides in farther, stretching me painfully.

"Please," I cry.

"Shhh, it's okay." His hand skims down my quivering belly and stops to knead and pinch my clit.

Art presses my face against the wall, kissing down the side of my neck as he fully impales me. My mouth opens in a silent scream. The pleasure and pain is exquisite. He groans, pausing for a moment before fucking my ass in deep long strokes. I close my eyes, losing myself in the whirlwind gaining momentum inside my body.

"See? It's not so bad," he murmurs.

I angle my head to capture Art's lips in a passionate kiss, causing his control to snap. He starts fucking me like a man possessed—wild and ferocious. My toes leave the floor with each savage thrust. Our moans of ecstasy and heavy breathing echo throughout the bedroom. The scent of sex permeates the air around us. My orgasm takes over my body with such intensity, I become incoherent. This feeling is beyond words. Art gives one final thrust, filling me with his cum. I slump against him when he frees me from the leather straps. He picks me up and carries me to the en suite bathroom. Art places me on unsteady legs before switching on the light. Damn, it's half the size of my apartment. Art grasps my hand and leads me to the shower stall, which takes up an entire wall. He slides the glass door open and turns the valve, then waits, allowing the water to heat. A large square stainless-steel structure is attached to the ceiling in the center of the stall, hanging from short beams.

"What is that called?"

"It's a rainfall shower head."

"I've never heard of it before."

"Then get prepared for a mind-blowing experience."

He pulls me inside with him, and hot water cascades over me, soothing my sore limbs. "This feels so amazing."

"It'll be the best shower you've ever had." He moves behind me, gliding a bar of soap over my breasts, then down my stomach.

"I think I can manage washing myself. Thank you very much."

"But I'll do it so much better," he murmurs, pinching my left nipple.

I drop my head back against his chest, groaning in rapture as he briskly circles the soap around my clit.

"Art!" I shout, digging sharp nails into his forearm as my climax tears through me, leaving me weak.

I slump against him, depleted and thoroughly sated.

"I told you I'd do it better."

Twenty minutes later, we lie together on the king-sized bed while my head rests on his chest.

"When did you open your nonprofit?"

"A year ago."

"That's an awesome way to honor Cole's memory."

"My long-term goal is to open multiple locations. Every child should be taught how to swim. Mason has been in the water since he was old enough to crawl. He's still not advanced, but he's getting there."

"Is he your son?"

"No, my brother. I'm his legal guardian."

"Where's your mom?"

"I don't know, nor do I give a fuck. Mason is better off without her. She became a millionaire after my father died and split."

"What about his father?"

"She wouldn't give up the bastard's name. Most likely some married rich piece of shit who kicked her to the curb once he found out she was pregnant."

"I'm sorry about your dad."

He shrugs his shoulder. "He was never the same after his stroke. Death was better for him."

"That's harsh."

He chuckles. "Hold on while I get my tiny violin."

"It's okay not to always be an asshole."

"But I'm so good at it." He pauses for a minute. "I can't help but wonder why you didn't reach out to let me know you were expecting. You couldn't possibly have known Trevor was the father."

"You're right, I didn't. I thought it was best not to contact you unless I was one hundred percent sure you were the father."

"I'm sure you were excited when you learned I wasn't, imagining you would live happily ever after with Trevor. Just so you know, I would never deny my flesh and blood no matter how much I hate the mother."

He latches onto my arm when I swing my legs over the side of the bed.

"Where do you think you're going?"

"I want you to take me home, now." I've had enough of his shit for one night.

He jerks me back. "I run this fucking show, not you. You're staying the night, so lie down and get comfortable."

I wonder how different things would be if Sebastian was Art's son.

ART

I feel disgusted with myself watching her delicate face as she sleeps. Thick eyebrows arch over slightly slanted eyes, small upturned nose, and thick soft pink lips— fucking perfection. She ensnared me in her spider's web after only one night of fucking, and my dumb ass was easy pickings. Shit, this fucking female will always drive me crazy. I should've thrown her out of my car when I realized who she was, but I'm fucking weak when it comes to Cin and always will be. My emotions resemble a bubbling volcano, unstable and prone to erupt unexpectedly. I want her, but I fucking hate her. My hands tremble as I think about causing her pain. Fuck forgive and forget. Anyone who crosses me will remain on my shit list forever, and she's number one. I want her to experience the same hurt she caused me. She became my salvation, helping me when no one else could. God, she made me so damn happy. I would've given her any fucking thing. Those last words she said to me eight years ago still haunt me. *You should've died the day you slit your wrists.* I was ready to devote my life to her, but that night changed everything. I visit Cole's grave on his birthday every year because of her. What makes her so goddamn special? There's absolutely nothing unique about her. I've fucked plenty of gorgeous women, from supermodels to actresses. I pull the comforter down her body, revealing the sexy dip in her back. My dick stands to attention. How the fuck can a back make me hard? I tug the comforter down farther, exposing her nakedness. She mumbles but remains asleep when I squeeze her delectable round ass—it's like touching cotton. I cover her with my large body, waking her up instantly.

"Stop! What are you doing?"

"I'm ready to ravage your pussy again," I say, entering her welcoming heat.

She wiggles beneath me, trying to get free. "I'm too sore."

I lay my forearm across the back of her neck, pushing her face into the mattress.

"I don't give a damn. You'll need a cane to walk after I'm done with you."

She may be a Cin, but I swear I'm in fucking heaven. Her sopping wet cunt greedily consumes my dick. I fuck her ruthlessly with no remorse, tearing through her already inflamed flesh—each stroke more brutal and powerful than the last. Her fingers dig into the bedding as she makes unintelligible sounds.

"If you fuck another man, I'll torture him before dissolving his remains in acid. And you won't escape my fury, oh no. I'll kill you too."

I explode as her sweet cunt milks my dick. Shit, this fucking female will always drive me crazy.

It's still dark outside when I wake in bed alone. Not bothering to put on any clothes, I go downstairs in search of Cin. If she ran, I'm going after her. I won't allow her to back out of our arrangement. I turn towards the kitchen when I hear a noise coming from that direction. I watch as she rummages through the cabinets, looking like sex incarnate in my shirt.

"What are you doing?"

She screams, spinning around, clutching a hand to her chest. "You scared me."

Her gaze traverses my naked form.

I smirk. "Do you like what you see?"

"How could I not? You have an amazing body."

Cin's eyes widen as I advance on her. I place both hands on the counter, caging her in.

"I'm hungry. There's nothing to eat here."

"This place is for fucking, not eating."

"You don't live here?"

"I have a mansion. No woman has ever been there."

"How many women have you fucked in that bed?"

"I don't keep track. Hell, I don't remember the last time the bedding was changed. Did you think you were special?"

I grab her wrist when she tries to slap me.

"Think really hard the next time you raise a hand to me because I hit back." I bend her wrist inwards.

"You're going to break it!" she screams.

I fling her arm away. "Remember what I said."

"Am I the only one required to be exclusive for the duration of our arrangement?"

"Damn fucking right."

"So, you can go stick your tongue and dick in whomever?"

"I recall you fucking me while in a relationship with Trevor. It doesn't feel good now that the shoe is on the other foot, huh?"

I tear open the shirt she's wearing, scattering buttons across the kitchen floor. "I'm hungry, but not for food."

I plant her naked ass on the counter and move between her luscious thighs. Bringing her breasts together, I suck on her pretty nipples, going from left to right, then back again, bringing them to hard points. She throws her head back, moaning in bliss as she threads her fingers through my hair, pushing me closer to her bountiful mounds. I descend to my knees, trailing kisses along the way. I spread her pussy lips to examine the paradise between her legs that brings out the psychotic motherfucker in me.

"Your pussy must be laced with cocaine."

This fucking upside-down triangle completely wrecks me. It's been less than forty-eight hours and she has me back under her spell. She's the only person on this planet that can reduce me to a state of madness, and I fucking hate her for it. I glide my tongue over the hood of her clit, then across, making an invisible A for Arthur's pussy. I grasp her thighs, opening them wider before latching onto her swollen nub and sucking rapidly. She comes in minutes, begging me to stop as she tries to twist away, but I continue the assault until another orgasm rips through her. My senses are filled with her. She's every-fucking-where. Sleep evaded me last night because of her. I lick my way up her quivering body, and my fucking God, the sight of her dripping pink pussy, flushed skin, and heavy-lidded gaze is enough to make me want to lock her away forever from the prying eyes of other men. I grip my engorged length, pausing at her center, but instead of pushing inside, I run the tip along her slit to play in the wetness gathered there before rocking forward, shaking like a little bitch. That's how powerful her affect is on me. Her cunt yields, accepting my invasion, and I lose myself in her out-of-this-world pussy, pounding into her relentlessly.

"You like mind-fucking me, driving me insane." It's an accusation.

"You think you're the only one suffering? I've been half dead since you," she says.

After hooking my arms behind her knees, I lift her from the counter and slam her back against the refrigerator. I roll my hips, pummeling into her tight sheath while our tongues intertwine, creating a sensual rhythm. Cin's pussy clamps down on my dick as she reaches climax. I swallow her scream of pleasure, filling her to overflowing with my thick cum. Drained of energy, I slide to the floor.

"Well, well, well—is there room for two more?"

I glance over my shoulder and see Josh standing there with a girl. I gave him the okay to bring his fucks here if the need arises, but right now isn't a good time.

"Cover yourself and stay behind me," I whisper as we move to our feet.

"Sorry, you'll need to go elsewhere tonight."

"Come on, there's plenty of—"

"Get the fuck out of here!"

"You never cared before. Now I'm curious to meet your lady friend." He walks forward.

"Don't come any closer," I demand. I don't want Josh anywhere near Cin.

"Let's go someplace else," the girl says, fidgeting.

"We will, sweetheart, after I see who's hiding behind my dear cousin."

"I swear if you don't leave right now, I'm going to kick your ass."

Cin steps to the side. "Hi, Josh."

His gaze snaps to her, then back to me.

"Get the fuck upstairs!" I shout, pushing her roughly.

"Prick!" she yells, running from the kitchen.

"What the fuck is she doing here?"

"That's none of your concern."

"I'll wait outside." The girl makes a hasty retreat.

"You're still obsessed with her," he says.

"I think it's fair to say I'm past that point."

"It's best to let sleeping dogs lie."

"I can't," I say.

He walks towards me until we're standing toe to toe. "Don't say I didn't warn you."

Cin

I lie on the bed, pissed off at Art's macho attitude. I only did what was necessary to prevent them from fighting. The air shifts when Art enters the bedroom. I can feel the danger emanating from him. It's almost suffocating. When I notice the belt in his right hand, I move to my knees, preparing for either fight or flight.

"W-what are you going to do?" I stutter.

"You disobeyed me. I instructed you to stay behind me and not to speak to another man. It's time for your ass whooping. Lie facedown on the bed."

"Fuck you." I roll to the opposite side of the bed, putting it between us when he moves towards me.

"It's going to be worse if I have to chase you," he says, walking around.

I crawl back across, racing to the bathroom and locking myself inside.

He bangs on the door. "Open the fuck up and take your beating like a woman."

"You're crazy if you think I'm going to be docile while you hit me with a belt."

"You can't stay in there all night."

Damn, he's right. What the hell am I going to do?

"I'm sorry, okay? I won't disobey you again."

"It's too late for apologies. Little pig, little pig, let me in."

"Kiss my ass!"

"Then I'll huff and puff and blow your house down."

He rains blow after blow on the door and splits it down the middle. I frantically search the bathroom, desperate for anything I can use as a weapon. Shit, there's nothing. After one more hit, he gains entry. I plaster myself to the wall, my heart in my throat.

"Here's Art."

"Let's talk about this like sensible adults."

He waves me forward. "Don't make me come get you."

I slowly walk towards him as if I'm complying with his command, but I make a run for it when I pass him. He catches me before I can even make it three steps and drags me to the bed.

"Damn caveman! Let me go!"

He tosses me onto my stomach, then drops his heavy body on top of mine to prevent any more escape attempts. He latches onto my wrist and handcuffs me to a bedpost. I crane my head, seeing more handcuffs dangling from the remaining three posts. I didn't notice them earlier. Once he has all my limbs secure, he leaves the bed.

"This is going to hurt me more than it's going to hurt you." He cracks the belt across my ass, hard and fast. It feels as if the skin is being torn from my body.

"Art, please! Stop!" I sob, tears leaking from my eyes.

"You. Will. Learn. To. Obey. Me." Each word is followed by a brutal strike more painful than the last.

After a few more hits, he's finally done. My wrists and ankles are released, but I lie there, hurting and in shock.

"Go downstairs and get dressed. We're going to breakfast."

Breakfast!

I whip my head in his direction. He stands with his back towards me, slipping on his pants. My control snaps and I launch myself at him. Not surprisingly, he gains the upper hand almost immediately, flipping me around and crossing my arms over my chest, leaving me immobile.

"I hate you," I sob, sagging against him.

"I explained the rules several times, but you chose to ignore them. To avoid punishment, I suggest you learn to fucking obey, because trust me, I can get a whole lot more creative with my discipline techniques."

"You don't care about hurting me?"

"No." He pushes me towards the door. "Be dressed by the time I get downstairs."

I won't be there, you fucking bastard.

"Cin."

I stop in the doorway, not turning around to face him.

"Don't run because I will give chase and imagine what I'll do once I catch you. And just in case that's not enough of an incentive, think about the better life you can provide for your son and mother with half a million dollars."

I glare at him from across the booth while he scarfs down his steak omelet like he doesn't have a care in the world. Meanwhile, I'm squirming, unable to keep still because my ass hurts like a motherfucker. My only solace is imagining dumping the contents of his coffee mug over his head.

"Eat."

"I can't eat," I hiss.

"Why not?" he asks, looking confused as he takes a bite of toast.

"I'm unable to sit comfortably."

"What does your mouth have to do with your ass?"

"Not a damn thing."

"Exactly, so eat your fucking food unless you want me tie a bib around your neck and feed you."

I snatch up the spoon, slamming it into the bowl of grits before ramming it into my mouth.

Damn! I hit my tooth!

"Are you okay? I'm pretty sure you'll need to see a dentist," he says, smirking.

I roll my eyes at him.

"You're asking for another spanking."

"I didn't do anything," I shrill.

"You rolled your eyes at me."

Calm down, you only have to deal with his bullshit for six months.

"I'm sorry, Daddy." I bat my eyelashes.

"Good girl." He pats the top of my head.

I pull my cell phone from my handbag to check if I have any missed phone calls from my mom. Surprisingly I don't, which is unusual because she's a worrier. I send her a text, but it doesn't go through.

"What the hell? My service is off, but I paid the bill."

"I had your number transferred to your new phone."

"What new phone?"

"The one I bought and had delivered to your apartment."

"You didn't have to do that."

"That piece of crap is outdated." He points his fork at my phone. "And the screen is cracked. Thank you is the proper response."

"Thank you."

"You're welcome. Your car has been delivered as well. The keys were given to your mother. It's nothing flashy. I kind of figured you would prefer something simple."

"You bought me a car?" I ask, incredulously.

No doubt my mom has a million questions for me.

"I did, but for my own selfish reasons."

"Which are?" I ask, taking a sip of orange juice.

"It'll be quicker for you to drive to me on your own versus waiting on a taxi."

"What about insurance, tags—"

"Everything has been taken care of."

"Okay." I shouldn't ask this next question, but I'm curious. "Do you and Josh live together?"

He sits forward, digging his fingernails into my knee. "Let's get one thing straight. You don't ask about

Josh. He is none of your fucking business. If you ever find yourself about to cross paths with him, it's in your best interest to take a fucking detour. Is that clear?"

"Crystal," I grit between clenched teeth. "Please remove your hand."

"I'm glad we understand each other." He leans back. "Be at my penthouse by eight tonight."

"I can't."

"What the fuck did you say?"

"I have to spend time with Sebastian. I can come Monday after work, but I can't stay the night."

"Fair enough, your son comes first."

This is the first battle I've won with him.

"Have you taken him to any of the theme parks yet?"

"No, I can't afford it."

"Take him this weekend. I'll purchase a season pass for your mother, Sebastian, and you. Mason already has one."

"That's not—"

"I only ask that you bring Mason along. He could use a friend."

"This is temporary. Do you think it's wise to schedule playdates? What if they become attached? I don't want them to get hurt."

"There's no reason why they can't remain friends when our arrangement ends. I would never mistreat

Sebastian. He has nothing to do with the issues between you and me."

I have no idea why, but I believe him.

I nod in understanding. "Sebastian has talked about going nearly every day since we moved here. He'll be very excited. My mom won't be able to go though."

"Why?"

"It's not a good idea because her migraines appear so suddenly."

"Your mother has three doctor's appointments scheduled this week. All are experts in their field and come highly recommended. One of them should be able to pinpoint the cause of her migraines."

"That was quick. Thank you so much."

Hopefully she'll have the chance to live a normal life. Her self-esteem took a major blow when she lost her eye. Being able to work will give her the boost she desperately needs.

"I'm keeping up my end of the deal. Make sure you do the same."

"I will."

Eleven

Cin

The front door swings open the moment I slide my key into the bottom lock. My mom stands in the doorway, tapping her foot with a hand on her hip.

"Good morning. I'm surprised you're up this early."

"Why didn't you tell me you were expecting deliveries last night?"

"Do you mind if I come inside first? Then I'll answer all your questions."

"Oh, sorry." She steps back, allowing me entry.

"I didn't know or I would've told you," I answer as I plop down on the sofa.

"It must be pretty serious between you and Adrian for him to give you such extravagant gifts. Do I hear wedding bells?" She sits beside me.

"He didn't buy me the cell phone or the car. We're not dating anymore."

"I don't understand. I thought everything was going great."

"We were only dating, nothing serious. It's run its course."

"Who bought you the phone and car? You can't afford to make those kinds of purchases."

"I have something to tell you, but you have to promise to hear me out."

"You're scaring me, Cin. What's going on?"

"Just have an open mind. Can you do that for me?"

"I'll try."

"I ran into Art the other day. He's the person who drove me home when my car broke down."

"Do you plan on seeing him again?" she asks with a worried frown on her face.

"Yes, but only as a friend."

My mom would choose to suffer for the rest of her days if she knew the details of our arrangement.

"You have to stay away from him."

"He's not the same person."

"People like him don't change. He's vindictive and unstable."

"He wants to make amends for what happened."

"How?"

"Art bought me the gifts."

"Give them back. We'll manage. We always do."

"He's already arranged for you to start seeing specialists this week."

"What?" The hopeful expression on her face is worth dancing with the devil.

"You can finally receive a diagnosis."

"But at what cost? I can't believe he's doing this out of the kindness of his heart."

"This is your opportunity to live a normal life."

"Mom!" Sebastian runs from the bedroom and jumps in my lap.

"Hi, handsome, did you sleep well?"

"Yes. I'm hungry."

"Well, a growing boy does need to eat. How about some pancakes for breakfast?"

He eagerly nods.

"Go take out the ingredients. I'll be right there."

"Okay." He runs into the kitchen.

"Please think about it," I plead. "You want me to forgive myself for what happened. This is how."

It was an underhanded move on my part for making that comment, but at least she'll be on board now.

ART

Thoughts of Cin have been on replay since dropping her off. I've spent the last several hours working out in my home gym. I should be past the point of exhaustion by now, but my body is a live wire. I swear she's a fucking virus, pumping through my veins. After having a taste of her again, there's no way in fucking hell I'll be able to let her go a second time. There's no point in denying it. Whether Cin likes it or not, she belongs to me. I'm going to have her on a leash so tight, she'll barely be able to breathe. I have six months to figure out how to keep her with me.

Damn.

This wasn't part of my quest for revenge. My T-shirt and shorts cling to my sweat-drenched body as I reach thirteen miles on the treadmill.

"There you are. Were you purposely dodging my calls?" Josh asks, coming into the room.

"Yep."

"We need to talk."

"I'm not interested in hearing whatever it is you have to say."

"You don't even know what I want to discuss." He stops in front of the treadmill.

"Don't treat me like an idiot."

"Then stop acting like one."

I jump off the treadmill and get in his face. "She's not a topic open for discussion."

"You're being fucking stupid."

I push him. "What I do is my fucking business! I don't need a damn babysitter!"

"Obviously you do!"

"You're walking on dangerous ground."

"What are your intentions for the little school teacher?"

"How the fuck do you know what she does for a living?"

"It wasn't hard to find out."

"Stay the fuck away from her, Josh. I mean it. If you go anywhere near her, I'll beat you to within an inch of your life."

"We had a rocky start, Art. Luckily, we finally came to an understanding. You would ruin that over some washed-up pussy?"

Before I realize what I'm doing, Josh is on his ass with a bloody mouth.

"I guess the answer is yes," he says, spitting blood onto the floor.

"You've been in Florida long enough. It's time for you to go home."

He stands. "I really need to explore between her legs so I can understand what has you so fucking crazy."

I headbutt him, sending him toppling on his ass again.

"Fuck! My nose! You motherfucking son of a bitch!"

"You deserved it."

"Damn, asshole. I'll have to cancel my date tonight. I can't show up looking like I was used as a punching bag."

"Not my problem. You should've kept that hole in your face shut. Look on the bright side, now you have a bloody nose to match your bloody mouth."

"So, this is how it's going to be?" he asks, glaring at me.

"Leave," I sneer, walking towards the exit. "You've overstayed your welcome."

There's no denying Cin has me by the balls. Fuck, I'm in too deep already.

Twelve

Cin

My lips form a mischievous smile as I answer Anneli's call. "Hello?"

I've been expecting a phone call since her shift ended an hour ago. I really should be in bed this late on a Sunday night, but instead I'm glued to the sofa, watching television while eating my weight in cereal.

"Tell me all the juicy details," she exclaims.

"I had a great day. Thank you for asking. How was work?" I say, placing my late-night snack on the floor.

"Awesome. Spill, I want to know everything."

"No time for small talk tonight?" I ask teasingly.

"How long are you going to leave me guessing?" Anneli whines.

"There's nothing to tell," I say nonchalantly.

"Oh, so you're really going to leave me hanging? I think it's time I advertise for a new best friend."

"Isn't that a bit drastic?" I laugh.

"Nope."

"Well, he's still a level-one asshole." I click the television off, then stretch across the soft cushions.

"Duh, that information isn't newsworthy. Come on. Give me something I can work with."

"He's already scheduled my mom to see specialists this week."

"That's amazing. I'm so happy for her."

"I had to convince her to go."

"Does she know about—"

"Are you crazy? She can never find out, so make sure you keep your mouth shut."

"I want what's best for her, just like you. At first I was on the fence about your decision, but I understand why you did it."

"Thank you."

"No problem, babe."

"He bought me a new car and cell phone."

"My goodness. How does it feel to live the lifestyle of the rich and fabulous?"

"Fabulous is something I could never be."

"Did you have sex with him?" she whispers conspiratorially.

"Sex is definitely too tame of a word to describe what we did."

She squeals in my ear. "Psychotic men fuck best."

"He owns my body."

"Damn girl, he must've fucked the shit out of you."

"He did, but it's more than that. When I was with him, it was like no time had passed between us at all. It's strange how something so wrong could feel so right. I promised myself I wouldn't let him get the best of me, that I would distance my emotions. I knew it was a lie. By the time this is over, I won't be the same. With him, I'm different."

"Don't give him that kind of power over you."

"He already has it. God, I'm so fucking pathetic."

"You're not."

"You remember how he was in high school. Multiply that by one million. He's so intense and terrifying. And his mood changes are unpredictable, but it doesn't lessen my desire for him."

My pussy weeps for him. Trained like a bitch in heat. No foreplay needed—his dick slides right in with no resistance.

"I'm afraid for you."

"Not as much as I am for myself."

"I led you straight to him by convincing you to move here."

"Stop it. I'm not going to let you blame yourself. The day I met him, a fuse was lit. Eight fucking years later, the fire is still blazing."

"Just end it. We can find some other way to help your mom."

"Even if I wanted to, he wouldn't let me."

"Shit."

"Look, don't worry about me. I'll be okay. I would follow him into hell if it meant a better life for my family. Let's change the subject. How are things going between you and Christian?"

"Great!" she answers too quickly.

"What happened?"

"I need to enroll in acting classes."

"And it still wouldn't help. I'm waiting."

"We've been fighting…" she trails off.

"Because of me?"

"No. Yes." She sighs. "He wants to understand your reasoning behind breaking up with Adrian, but obviously I can't tell him. We haven't spoken today."

"I'm so sorry. I'm always fucking up other people's lives." I walk to the kitchen and put my bowl and spoon in the sink.

Socializing with me should be considered a health hazard.

"He'll cool down in a few days."

"Maybe I should call Adrian and be up front with him."

"Definitely not. This is the type of secret you take to your grave. Tell no one."

"Christian probably thinks I'm a bitch now," I groan, leaning against the counter.

"He'll get over it, so will Adrian."

"Have you talked to him?"

"Stop torturing yourself. What's done is done."

"You're right. I'm not going to dwell on it."

"Good. I'm going to let you get to sleep so you can be prepared for those bad-ass kids in the morning." She laughs.

"Don't remind me. I'll talk to you later."

"All right, babes."

Instead of going to bed, I plant my ass back on the sofa and turn the television on. My body is too active to settle down for sleep. I slide my hand between my legs, thinking of him. There'll be nothing left of me after six months of Art.

ART

I glance at my cell phone lying on the desk when it begins to ring for the eighth time in the span of ten minutes. My grandfather is annoyingly persistent. The goddamn bastard irritates the fuck out of me, so I avoid conversation with him at all costs unless it's absolutely necessary. Grimacing in irritation, I answer my cell when it rings for the ninth time, just in case there's an emergency.

"Yeah."

"Finally," he says dramatically.

"What do you want?"

"Joshua told me you've been seeing that girl from North Carolina."

The piece of shit actually ran and snitched on me. Tattletale-ass motherfucker. He's due for a beatdown the next time I see him. I've warned him several times to stop discussing my business with our grandfather.

"I thought something major was happening since you called back-to-back," I deadpan.

"Leave her alone. You have women falling at your feet."

"But they're not who I want."

"Have you forgotten about her treachery?"

"I haven't." How can I when the knife is still protruding from my fucking back?

"She's going to make a fool of you again."

"Your concern is very touching, but I can handle her."

"Are you sure? You spiraled out of control last time."

I was naïve to trust in her so explicitly, but that was then, and this is now. It'll be a cold day in hell before I let her into my heart again. "Stay out of my personal matters!"

"Tell me you're at least using protection."

"I fucked her raw and came in her more than several times."

"Is she on birth control?"

"She isn't."

"What if she gets pregnant?" he shouts.

"Then that'll be my fucking business. Now, if you don't have anything important to discuss, enjoy the rest of your day."

"You're making—"

I disconnect the call.

Leaning back against the chair, I imagine Cin's midsection swollen with my baby. The idea isn't repulsive. In fact, I like it very much. I immediately shut down that line of thinking. What the fuck is wrong with me? The mother of my children will not be a two-faced backstabbing bitch. I know this, but still refuse to use protection and will be painting her insides with my cum this evening. I've been looking forward to seeing her again, even arriving at the hotel earlier than usual, so I can leave at a decent hour just to be with her. I'm a fucking idiot.

Cin

Another sexy dress, panty set, and stilettos were not waiting for me when I arrived home from work, like I expected. The only communication I received from Art is a text instructing me to wear my hair down. He didn't mention if we were going out or staying in, so I opted to wear leggings, an oversized T-shirt, and flip-flops. I check the time on my cell phone as the elevator stops at the penthouse level. I'm thirty minutes early. I thought about making a grand entrance by purposely arriving five minutes late, but self-preservation won over rebellion. My heart beats faster, excitement and trepidation battling for domination as the door slides open. I'm surprised to see rose petals on the floor, leading into the foyer. If I didn't know better, I'd think Art is attempting to be romantic. I follow the path upstairs to the bedroom. A contraption that wasn't here on Saturday hangs from the ceiling. The rose petals end at the foot of the bed where I find a blindfold and a note.

I want you naked, in the center of the bed, legs spread, with the blindfold on. Place your hands behind your head where they must remain or you will be punished. You have two minutes to comply.

Sincerely,

Your Owner aka Pussy Connoisseur

He's fucking with me. I pick up the blindfold, eyeing it suspiciously. What adventures will he take me on tonight? Not willing to get on his bad side, I quickly shed my clothes and climb on the bed, then reluctantly cover my eyes. I'm on alert, turning my head towards the slightest noise. Low music fills the room. I'm unable to hear any movement at all. The suspense has me on edge. Art is the king of mind games, twisting me into knots but easing his hold before I snap. I move my hands, startled by a soft caress at my hip. Maybe a feather. A stinging slap is delivered to my leg.

"The punishment will be more severe if you disobey again. Put your fucking hands where they belong."

I immediately follow the command given.

The bed dips with Art's added weight. I shake as he skims the feather along my body, but the true test of my willpower starts when he ventures to my most intimate area. I squeeze my legs shut, unable to bear it any longer, but he pries them back open. His fingers replace the feather, sliding through my slick pussy.

"Have you ever squirted?" His lips brush against my ear as he asks the question.

"No," I answer breathlessly.

"You must've only fucked amateurs after me. What a shame."

Maybe that's part of the reason why I never made an effort to date. No man could ever measure up to him.

"I've learned a few tricks over the years. You're in for a sexual awakening." He kisses my neck.

I tremble, overwhelmed by the violent storm brewing inside me.

"Do you know where your G-spot is?"

I shake my head.

"It's located about three inches inside your pussy, on the front wall."

I moan as he slowly penetrates my wet pussy with his finger.

"You're so tight," he murmurs.

He rapidly moves in and out of my quivering cunt. A tingling sensation consumes me within minutes.

"Stop. I have to pee," I shout.

I try to sit up, but he lays his upper body across my chest to keep me in place.

"It's not pee. Just relax and let go," he says softly.

"Please stop," I sob, struggling against him.

I'll be so embarrassed if I pee on myself.

His fingers become more urgent until the damn breaks and liquid pours from my throbbing pussy. The feeling is indescribable.

"Oh my God," I scream and then… nothing.

I awake to Art calling my name. The blindfold no longer covers my eyes.

"What happened?"

"You lost consciousness."

I just received the most powerful orgasm I've ever had. It's scary as fuck but exhilarating.

"There's more."

A naked Art leaves the bed, pulling me with him. He leads me to the contraption hanging from the ceiling.

"What is this?"

"It's your ride for tonight."

He handcuffs my wrists taut above my head, then guides my thighs into the sling, leaving me suspended off the floor in a sitting position. My legs are spread wide to the point of being painful, stretching muscles I haven't used in a long time. Art steps away for a few minutes but returns with lubricant and an oval-shaped object.

"I bought this anal plug especially for you."

I tense when he rubs the gel between my cheeks.

"Remember, it's better if you relax."

I whimper as he pushes the anal plug into my ass until I'm completely impaled.

"I have another surprise for you."

Art steps away again, this time returning with a vibrator. He clicks it on then moves it over my clit in circular motions. I moan, surging against the handcuffs.

"Come for me."

My orgasm hits like a wrecking ball, transporting me to a world of ecstasy and carnal perfection.

"What are you doing to me?" I whisper.

"The same thing you're doing to me, driving you in-fucking-sane."

Art glides his dick through my drenched slit before entering my pulsating depths.

"Fuck," he growls.

Both of my holes are filled to the brim. And with the vibrator still on my clit, I'm losing touch with reality. His thick length plunges in and out, pounding into my pussy. I reach orgasmic bliss, squirting again as tears roll down my cheeks. He's going to fucking destroy me. Who am I kidding? He already has. I had no idea sex could be like this. There's no way he's human—more like a supernatural creature wielding dangerous powers.

"Shit," he groans, giving one more bone-jarring thrust.

Art falls to his knees, resting his cheek against my thigh for a few minutes before standing.

He pulls the anal plug from my ass then helps me down and carries me to the bed. I close my eyes, rolling to the side as soon as I'm placed on the mattress. I'm exhausted. Sex with Art drains all my strength. He holds me close as I drift off to sleep.

I wake up to Art's warm lips trailing kisses down my back.

"Mmmmm." I roll over.

"Finally, I have your attention." He kisses my lips.

"What time is it?"

"A little after nine."

"I have to get home," I mumble.

"Have you eaten dinner?"

"No, I didn't want to be late and face the wrath of his highness."

He chuckles. "His highness—I like it. Moving forward, that's how you'll refer to me."

"In your dreams," I scoff.

I enjoy our playful banter. It takes me back to a time when we were inseparable. How I miss those days.

"I'll feed you before you leave. What do you want?"

"Egg foo young."

"What the fuck is that?"

"It's a Chinese dish."

"I never heard of it, but I rarely eat Chinese."

"It's really good. You should try it."

"What's in it?"

"It depends. You can have chicken, beef, shrimp, or veggies with eggs. Shrimp egg foo young is my favorite."

"Egg and shrimp do not go together."

"Hey, don't knock it until you try it."

"How about Italian?"

"Be adventurous and try something different."

"Fine."

When Art Falls: Living in Cin

ART

Cin sits to my left at the glass table, filling my paper plate with rice and the egg concoction before serving herself. I frown in disgust, wishing I'd never let her talk me into ordering Chinese.

"That scowl will become permanent if you keep it on your face long enough."

"Remember, you chose this if I get sick."

"You'll be perfectly fine, I promise."

Well it's now or never. I grab my fork, preparing to dig in.

"Wait."

"What?"

She pulls a container from the bag. "You can't eat it without adding gravy."

"It's bad enough you talked me into eating eggs with shrimp, but now you want to throw gravy in the mix too? I'll probably be on the toilet for days."

She laughs—the sound melodic and soothing. No wonder people "Cin" every day. It's irresistible… addictive.

"Dramatics don't become you." She pours a brown sauce over my food.

"Go ahead, take a bite. I'll be your sex slave for six months if it isn't one of the best dishes you've ever tasted." She grins. "Oh, wait a minute. I'm already your sex slave."

"You're so funny," I say sarcastically.

"Thank you very much. I'm on every night at seven."

I take a tentative bite. "This isn't so bad. Actually, it tastes pretty good."

"I hate to say I told you so, but…"

"No need to rub it in."

"I made a doctor's appointment, so I'll be on birth control soon."

"Cancel it."

"Why?"

"I already made you an appointment."

"I prefer to choose my own doctor."

"She's one of the best gynecologists in Florida and I'll be footing the bill."

"When is the appointment?"

"Thursday, at four o'clock."

"Where?"

"It's close to where you live. I'll text you the address later."

She brushes her thumb across my chin. "You have a little gravy here."

I catch her digit in my mouth, circling my tongue around it. "Cin and gravy tastes better."

She clears her throat. "Tell me about Mason."

"He's a good kid, eager to learn and smart as a whip. I'd do anything for him. But sometimes he's a little depressed."

"Why?" She bites into an egg roll.

"He wants a mother and father. That's something I can never give him. It makes me feel helpless."

She grasps my hand and squeezes reassuringly. "I completely understand how you feel. Sebastian asks about his dad all the time. I'll explain everything to him when he's older."

She's a black widow, coaxing me into her web only to devour me when I least expect it. I know it's a trap, but my dumb ass will follow her—needing her, even though it'll end in my demise. Goddammit, it wasn't supposed to be like this.

"Sebastian and I can hang out with Mason this weekend. We're going to have a great time."

Fuck that, I'm not letting her lure me into a false sense of security again. I take her paper plate and place it on the floor beside my foot. She glances at me in confusion.

"What are you waiting for? Get on your knees and finish your dinner."

"Are you serious?"

"As a heart attack. Get on the fucking floor."

"I'm full."

She screams in agony when I grab her index finger and apply pressure. "Do you want me to break it?"

"No!" she wails.

"Then you know what to do."

She hurriedly gives in to my command.

"Good girl," I say, petting the top of her head. "But no dessert after dinner, since you didn't obey right away."

The anger rolls off her in waves and it's exactly what I need from her. Fuck the kind, caring Cin. She makes me vulnerable when I need to remain strong. Her rage feeds my beast.

"Eat!" I shout.

Her body begins to shake. Good, her control is slipping. Come on, give me a reason. My hands twitch, ready to react instantly should she take it to the next level. *Fucking do it*, I silently beg. She picks up her plate and smashes it in my face.

Yes, now the monster will come out to play.

I latch onto her throat and lift her clear off the floor. Her eyes don't reflect fear, oh no. She's pissed. She scratches at my chest, drawing blood. I swipe my arm across the table, knocking what's left of our dinner to the floor before slamming her down. The glass cracks but doesn't shatter.

"You think you're tough enough to take me on?"

"I hate you." Tears spring into her eyes.

"What I feel for you is beyond hate."

I free my dick, then savagely thrust inside her, putting all my strength behind each stroke. I fuck her with an intensity that scares even me. Her screams ring through my ears, adding fuel to the burning inferno brewing in my body. The glass cracks more with each punishing blow. Her pussy clamping down on my length sends me over the edge. Shouting out, I surge forward at breakneck speed, exploding at the same time the table shatters. We fall to the floor on top of the broken glass.

"You're a nightmare I can't wake from," I say, peering into her eyes.

"And yet you keep falling asleep."

Cin

I key in the code given to me by Art, then drive through the gate. Palm trees line either side of the stone driveway leading to the magnificent estate. Coming to a stop, I survey my surroundings. What could one man and a child need with such a massive place? I look back at the sleeping boys. We got to the park when it opened and didn't leave until five. They're dead to the world, exhausted from today's activities. So am I. My feet are killing me. I'll definitely need to soak in Epsom salt. We only went to one theme park, but we'll visit more soon. Sebastian and Mason are kindred spirits. I'm sure they'll want to spend all of their free time together now. Art brought Mason to my apartment early this morning. It was awkward having him in the tiny space. Mom doesn't hold any ill will towards him, but she's still concerned about us reconnecting. They made small talk, but it was forced, so it was a relief when he left. He called once to check on Mason and to ask if I could drop him off at home instead of taking him back to my place. I agreed but was a bit shocked he gave me his address since he's been very vocal about never supplying that information to any woman.

I send a text to Art, letting him know I'm outside. He appears within a few minutes. My eyes roam over his sweaty form. He must've been working out. His T-shirt clings to the amazing chest I've become all too familiar with. I love to rub my hands over his hard flesh while he fucks me into oblivion. With each thrust, his muscles bunch and strain, creating a mesmerizing sight. The tattoo covering his right arm comes to life, the flames dancing with each movement as if the image is going to leap from his flesh. Physically, he's absolute perfection. Mentally, he's one messed-up human being. Yet I still yearn for him. His psychosis is rubbing off on me. He demanded I make myself available Wednesday night, then again on Friday, and I went willingly. The thought of denying him never entered my mind. Our fucking is a battle, the fight for control and survival always epic, but the war is never won. There's a moment of peace after we climax and bask in the glow of carnal bliss. We part with wounds, only to start anew and repeat the cycle. The cuts on my back from the glass are still healing and my pussy still aches from the brutal onslaught he's delivered between my legs.

I step out of the car. "Hi."

He stalks towards me until we're only inches apart.

"I hope he wasn't too much trouble for you."

"No, not at all. Mason's a sweet kid. He and Sebastian got along perfectly."

"Good."

His gaze is so damn intense I'm surprised I haven't melted into a puddle.

"They had a blast today. Thanks for making this possible for Sebastian."

"No problem."

"I didn't want to wake Mason. The little guy is worn out. Maybe you should carry him inside?"

"I could try, but he'll probably wake up."

He doesn't make a move, just continues to pin me with his unwavering stare.

"If it were just you and me out here, I'd fuck you where you stand."

A small whimper escapes my mouth, because damn if those words didn't cause me to wet my panties. He reaches his long arm out and clutches the back of my neck to bring me forward for a mind-numbing kiss. I melt into him, wishing we were alone too.

"Art!" Mason shouts.

We jump apart.

Mason throws his arms around his big brother's hips.

"I had so much fun with Sebastian! He's my new best friend."

"You should be ready for a bath and bed."

"No, I'm not tired," he huffs.

Sebastian wakes up and climbs out of the car too.

Art rubs the top of his head. "Hey, buddy. I heard you guys had an awesome time."

"We did," Sebastian replies with excitement.

They animatedly regale Art with stories of today's events. He's a totally different person around the boys. The transformation is amazing.

"Okay, it's time for us to head home," I say.

"Please don't go," Mason pleads as his bottom lip trembles.

"I'm sure Cin wants to rest after the long day she's had."

"But you promised to bake us a cake," Sebastian says.

"And you said we could be your helpers," Mason adds.

They're laying on the guilt real thick.

"Only if it's okay with Art," I say, looking at him.

"Sure. Everything needed to bake a cake should be in the fridge and pantry. If not, I'll run to the store."

"Shall we get started?" I ask.

Both boys squeal in delight, running towards the door.

ART

This is the happiest I've ever seen Mason. Cin sits beside him as he blends the ingredients together with the hand mixer. The expression on his face is priceless. For the last fifteen minutes I've observed her interactions with him from my seat at the kitchen island. She's caring, attentive, and patient. There's no doubt in my mind she'd be an amazing mother to him. If she could be bottled up and taken three times a day, all the damaged kids in the world would be healed.

"Sebastian, are you done buttering the pan?" she asks.

"Yep."

"Great, it's baking time." She switches the mixer off.

"I want sprinkles," Mason says.

"There weren't any in the pantry, but I'll be sure Marisa adds it to the grocery list," I say.

"Okay," he says with disappointment. "When will the cake be ready?"

"Forty-five minutes, then it'll need to cool for a bit," she answers, pouring the batter into the pan.

"That's going to take forever," he pouts.

"It'll be done before you know it," I say. "How about you take Sebastian to your room?"

I need some alone time with Cin.

"I have a lot of cool stuff to show you." He grabs Sebastian's hand, pulling him towards the door.

"So, who's Marisa?" Cin walks across the kitchen.

"Do I detect jealousy in your voice?"

"Absolutely not, I'm just curious."

I position myself behind her as she bends over to put the pan into the oven. "Liar."

I grab her throat and yank her against my chest. She lets out a low sexy moan as my hand pushes underneath her shorts to play between her legs.

"We can't. The boys could come back at any minute."

"Let's go to my bedroom."

"No. They might come looking for us."

"My room is soundproof and I'll lock the door."

"It's still too risky."

I pull my hand from her shorts and bring it to my nose, inhaling deeply. The smell of Cin's sweet earthy essence nearly makes me come. Fuck it. I'm not waiting. I need her now.

I tug her into the pantry.

"What are you doing?"

"I want my dick buried in your pussy in the next three minutes."

I drop to my knees, yanking her bottoms and panties down her legs. "I'll be quick." I bury my face in her cunt, tongue-fucking her.

"Oh my God," she moans, gripping my hair.

I slide my tongue to her clit, then penetrate her center with two fingers. Her body shakes uncontrollably as my fingers move. Liquid pours from her center to form a puddle on the floor. I stand, guiding her right thigh around my waist. I pull my hard length free and fill up her dripping-wet pussy.

"Cin," I say, resting my forehead against hers.

She places a soft kiss on my lips. "I think I'm falling in love with you again." Her words anger me because goddamn it I want her love. I move my hips, fucking her in a frenzy. This isn't lovemaking or even sex. Those words are too simplistic to describe this fever that burns between us. This is…

Armageddon.

"Your love is tainted, so keep it." The raw emotion in my voice is unmistakable.

Her nails dig into my back as her pussy clamps down on me.

It's a wonderful torment.

I shout, emptying my cum inside her pussy.

Cin

For the last couple of weeks, Art and I have been seeing more and more of each other. Our arrangement had a rocky start, but we've found common ground. He's still bossy as hell. Unfortunately, that'll never change. We've actually been on a few dates and sometimes we even have outings with the boys. I lie in bed, preparing to take a nap after being at the swimming pool all morning. Sebastian looks forward to going to Kids That Swim every weekend. Adrian no longer volunteers there, which is for the best. It would make for an uncomfortable situation. Mom is doing really well now. The doctor ordered an X-ray for her and discovered she had a prolapsed disc in her neck which was causing cervicogenic headaches. It's rare, but she needed to have surgery due to nerve compression. The injury occurred when the top of her head hit the wall from the impact of Trevor's boot. The emergency room doctor said she had a concussion and sent her packing. This could have been discovered a long time ago had the previous doctors done their due diligence. She has physical therapy on Mondays and Thursdays, and her doctor said she'll be fully recovered within several weeks.

My phone rings.

"Hello?"

"I'm attending a charity dinner. You're going as my date," Art says.

He never asks, always demands.

"Maybe I already have plans."

"Don't fucking play with me, Cin."

"Why am I just being told about this? Some notice would've been appreciated."

"I'm sending a car for you at six. Have your ass ready to go."

"What should I wear?"

"I transferred some money into your account."

"Of course you have my account number," I say dryly.

"The hair stylist will be at your place at four and the makeup artist at five."

"What about my mom? She's still recovering from surgery so can't be left alone with Sebastian for too long."

"The aide will be there before you leave." He ends the call.

Damn, he has everything covered. I click open the bank app to check my account balance. Holy fuck, he deposited five thousand dollars.

I dial the number of the one person I know who is an expert in style.

"Hello?" Anneli answers.

"I need your help."

"What happened? Did Art do something? I'll kick his fucking ass."

I laugh. "So, you're ready to slay the dragon for little ole me."

"You're damn straight. I'm going for the eyes first."

"O-M-G. You're a complete mess."

"I know I am, but you still love me."

"I do."

"So, what's up?"

"I need to go shopping."

"Where is Cin and what have you done with her? I knew there was some truth to the *Invasion of the Body Snatchers* movie!"

"I'm being serious! I have to buy a dress."

"Give me a second."

I hear movement on the other end of the phone.

"What's that noise?"

"I'm opening the window."

"What for?"

"To see if pigs are flying, because I never thought I'd hear you say those words. Or maybe I should check to see if hell has frozen over."

"Are you going to help me or not?" I ask, exasperated.

"Have some patience. I'm in shock at the moment."

"Are you done, drama queen?"

"Not quite yet. I need a few more minutes."

"While you're recovering, I'm going to head to the mall."

"Don't you dare. You can't be trusted to shop on your own."

"Well, let's go. I don't have that much time."

"Where are you going?"

"Art basically demanded I go as his date to a charity event."

"The lines are becoming blurred between you two."

"It's like we're in a relationship."

"This arrangement is a means to an end. It's an illusion."

"I know."

"Don't lose sight of your goal. I hate to see you get hurt."

I'm already in too deep, but I can't tell Anneli that. What the hell am I going to do once it's over?

"It's fine. I know what I'm doing." Maybe I'll believe the lie if I say it enough.

"Please tell me you're on birth control."

"I'm on the Depo shot."

I don't trust myself to take pills every day on time.

"Good. What's your spending limit?"

"Five thousand dollars."

Anneli lets out a long whistle. "We're going to have so much fun."

"It's already noon, shit. I have to be back home by four."

"I got this. I'll be there in twenty."

"See you then."

ART

I'm breaking my own damn rules. I hadn't planned on inviting Cin tonight. What the hell am I thinking? I've been treating her like she's my fucking girlfriend, and Mason has become attached to her and Sebastian. It'll be a shock to everyone here for sure, since I've never brought a date to any of these functions in the past. I'm attempting to be sociable with the group at the table, but

I'm bored to death and not listening to a word being said. I sit between Leonard and Damon. The former owns several nightclubs across Florida, and the latter is the heir to Lux International Airlines. I made the mistake of accepting an invitation to Leonard's club once, and he's been asking to hang out again every time we've run into each other since. The two are best friends. I guess they're looking to turn their duo into a trio, but I'm far from interested. Josh hit the streets with them almost daily during his stay. I only came tonight because, despite being a prick, I believe in contributing to a noble cause, and paying fifteen thousand per plate is pennies to me.

"So, what do you say?" Damon asks.

"About?"

"Coming to my birthday party at Opulence."

One of Leonard's establishments.

"I can't make it."

"I didn't tell you a date."

"When is it?"

"Next Saturday."

"I'm busy."

"You should come. It'll be closed to the public and the most beautiful women in Orlando will be there." Damon wags his eyebrows.

The only woman on my radar is Cin.

"Oh my, who is that?" Leonard asks.

I follow the line of his vison to see who he's referring to and my jaw drops. Not many things leave me speechless, but the sight of Cin coming towards me takes my fucking breath away. The simple, elegant black dress clings to her sexy curves. The V-neckline plunges low, showcasing her beautiful cleavage, and as she walks, the long slit going up her right leg reveals her thigh. Her long silky curls bounce with every step she takes. And my God, she's actually wearing heels without fumbling all over the damn place. A beautiful smile lights up her face when her eyes land on me.

"That's who I'm taking home tonight," Leonard says.

"Actually, she'll be going with me." Damon grins.

"Care to place a wager?" Leonard counters.

"That's my date, so the both of you need to fuck off."

Leonard scoffs. "Yeah right."

I stand when she reaches me. "You look gorgeous."

She blushes. "Thank you. I'm a real-life Cinderella."

"Oh shit. He's serious," I hear Damon say.

"You're in her seat," I say to Leonard.

He holds his hands up in surrender before standing and pulling out the chair for Cin.

I bump him out the way. "I got it."

She sits down. "Aren't you going to introduce me to your friends?"

"No."

"Hey, don't be like that," Leonard says.

"You're being rude," Cin whispers.

I glower at her. I'm about five seconds away from flipping the fucking table over. It was a mistake to invite her. Their eyes roam over her like she's a big fat juicy steak.

"My name is Leonard and he's Damon."

"Cin."

"That's a beautiful name," he says, kissing the back of her hand, "for a beautiful woman."

I feel the monster beating at me, trying to break free.

"It's short for Cinnamon."

"I love cinnamon. It's spicy with an unexpected sweetness. I eat it on practically everything."

"Watch your fucking mouth." I scowl.

"Chill, man," Damon says.

"Talk to her again, and I'll knock your teeth down your throat."

"It's okay," Cin says.

"Afraid of a little competition?" Leonard asks, smirking.

"You're not on my level and you couldn't make it there even if you borrowed an airplane from Damon.

But I tell you what—when I'm done with her, she's all yours."

Shocked gasps come from the occupants sitting around the table. It seems we've gained an attentive audience.

"Art," Cin says, horrified.

"She's open to spreading her legs for money."

"You fucking bastard."

"The truth is a hard pill to swallow, isn't it?"

"Cinnamon tastes best when you put it directly on your tongue." She licks her top lip while looking at Leonard.

I grip her arm, yanking her from the chair. "It's time for us to go."

"You're hurting me."

A hand clutches my shoulder. "Let her go."

I swing around, grabbing the front of Leonard's shirt. "Touch me again and you're dead."

"Gentlemen, please. This isn't the place for this," an older man says.

"You don't have to go with him. I'll take you home," Leonard offers.

"She knows who her bread and butter is." I glare at her. "You better fall in place behind me."

I head towards the exit. She'll always be a fucking whore, and I won't forget that again.

Cin

I can't believe he embarrassed me like that. It's difficult to keep my tears at bay. How can he make me feel special one moment and in the next treat me as if I'm a piece of shit? I follow him out the door into heavy rain. The night was pleasantly mild when I arrived, but now the wind is blowing and thunder cracks across the turbulent sky. The storm mirrors my emotions, taking me back to the night we were reunited.

Art gives a ticket to the valet. "Make it quick."

"Yes, sir."

"Asshole! You made all those people think I'm a hooker!"

He clasps my jaw. "Shut your fucking mouth."

"I won't back down from you tonight." I'm tired of his bullshit. If he wants a fight, I'll give him one.

"You'll be dealt with soon enough."

"I despise you."

But I love him too. My heart calls to his—it can't beat without him. We continuously stake along the thin line between love and hate.

"I fucking hate you too. Now get in the damn car," he says, flinging me away.

I settle in the car and buckle the seatbelt, mentally preparing myself for what's coming.

The tires squeal as he speeds off.

"Slow down!"

"You want to fuck him?"

"What?"

"You heard me!"

"That question doesn't deserve an answer."

"You were flirting with him!"

"That was after you started acting like a damn idiot!"

He turns onto the highway, traveling close to a hundred miles per hour.

"You're going to get us killed!"

"Maybe I should put us both out of our fucking misery."

He jerks the steering wheel left, driving over the median strip.

"What the hell are you doing?" I scream.

He speeds straight towards oncoming traffic. Motorists honk their horns, swerving out of the way to avoid a car accident.

"You're a lunatic!"

"You made me look like a fucking fool!"

"I'm sorry!" I'll say anything to get him to stop this madness. I lose control of my bladder, peeing in my panties a little when we nearly have a head-on collision. I've never been so afraid in my life.

"Since you want to behave like a slut, I'll treat you like one."

I've seen Art livid plenty of times, but this is beyond that. The sense of danger within the small confines of the car is suffocating. I can almost taste the fear in my mouth. Should I be scared for my life?

Art crosses back over the median and takes the next exit. He jerks the wheel, turning onto a dark, deserted street where he parks and jumps out of the car. I think about making a run for it, but he'll catch me in seconds. When he comes around to the passenger door, I hit the locks.

"Open this fucking door right now!"

I shake my head.

"It'll be hell to pay if you don't."

I flip him the bird.

"Fine. You want to play, let's go."

He walks away, disappearing into the night. I frantically search the surrounding area for any sign of him, but I can't see anything through the rain. I climb into the driver's seat, relieved I only have to push a button to start the engine. I'll face his wrath later for leaving him stranded, but right now I need to get away. Before I can put my plan in motion the passenger-side window is shattered. A very pissed off Art stands there, holding a brick. He reaches inside the car, twisting my hair in his hand. I scream bloody murder as he hauls me through the window. Jagged pieces of glass pierce my flesh. He laughs at my attempt to fight him off—the sound maniacal and frightening.

"It's amusing you think you can escape me," he sneers. "I'm stronger than you'll ever be."

Art savagely tears at my dress and panties until I'm left only in heels, completely exposed to the elements.

"I'll take whatever I want from you and there's nothing you can do about it." He moves his hand between my legs. "And right now, I want this." He rubs his nose against my cheek.

Cold raindrops beat against my heated skin. I scratch at his chest and bite his shoulder. He wraps his hand around my neck and shakes me like a rag doll.

"If you know what's good for you, you'll keep your goddamn teeth to yourself."

"Fuck you!" I shout.

"It makes my dick hard when you talk dirty."

He drags me to the front of the car and slams me down on the hood. I immediately stand, but he seizes the back of my neck and slams me down once more.

"If you move again, I'm going to take you back to my penthouse, handcuff you to the bed, and whip the skin off your ass."

He'll do it, so I stay put. Art positions himself behind me, pushing my legs apart with his foot.

"Someone might see us."

"Then let's give them a show."

He thrusts forward, fully sheathing his dick inside me. My eyes flutter closed, drowning in the feeling of him. Each time we fuck, he takes me higher and higher. When I finally fall, every bone in my body will break and I'll never heal from the irreversible damage. After this is over, he will move on with his life while I'll be permanently disabled.

"You belong to me. This pussy belongs to me," he growls.

My hard nipples slide over the wet metal as he pummels my pussy. Art always takes me on a sexual odyssey, leaving me desperate for more and impatient for what new heights he'll transport me to. Thunder lights up the sky the exact moment I come.

"Cin!" Art shouts, finding his own release.

All my life I've been made to believe love between a man and a woman should be sweet and tender. For Art and me, that couldn't be further from the truth. It's intimidating, untamed, and filled with pain. Even so, I wouldn't change the hurt for anything. We have no business being together. It's obvious we bring out the worst in each other, but my world doesn't work without him in it. It's ablaze and I'm going to watch it fucking burn.

ART

My obsession with Cin has spanned nearly a decade. Sometimes I curse the fates that allowed us to meet again, and other times I praise them for bringing her back into my life. We're almost two-and-a-half months into our arrangement and my mind is made up. I'm keeping her, even if she wants out. I've done something unforgivable to ensure she remains by my side. She can hate me, but there'll be no turning back. I started following her, like a jealous husband. I'm paranoid she'll cheat. If she does, someone is going to die. I'm waiting in the parking lot where she works for track practice to end. I drove a car she has never seen before, to catch her unaware. I like to watch how she behaves when I'm not around.

A group of kids emerge from the back of the school. Cin trails after them with a man walking beside her. They're too close together for my liking. My anger skyrockets when she grabs his shoulder and laughs at something he said. Who the fuck is this asshole? She's breaking the rules by speaking with him, and for that she's going to pay. I get out of the car, ready to kick some ass.

Her eyes widen at my approach. "What are you doing here?"

"Am I interrupting your planned rendezvous with this fucker?" I look the man up and down.

"Art, don't do this here," she says in a panic.

"Is there a problem?" the man says, stepping in front of her.

He doesn't realize how much danger he's in.

"No, everything is okay." She tries to move around him, but he holds out his arm. "I'll see you tomorrow."

She's trying to save the dummy, but he's not too bright.

"I can call the police if this guy is bothering you."

I grip her arm, jerking her to my side. My fist flies when he reaches for her, punching the bastard in the face and knocking him to the ground.

"Lights out, motherfucker."

"Jerry!" Cin moves to go to his side, but I tighten my hold on her. "We have to help him."

"Fuck him."

"Art, the kids are watching."

Fuck, and they're recording with their cell phones. This will be all over social media and news outlets within the hour. My grandfather might even make an appearance in Florida after this fuckup. Damn, this woman makes me do stupid shit.

"He needs an ambulance."

"Your lover will be fine," I say, hauling her ass to my car.

"Our relationship is purely professional!"

"You're a fucking liar."

"He's just a colleague. We were talking, that's all."

"Why were you walking so close to him? There's something more going on. I'm not fucking stupid!"

"Obviously you are! Why won't you listen to me?"

I open the door and shove her inside.

"What about my car?"

"It'll be picked up later," I say before slamming the door.

"Your little stunt is probably going to get me fired!" she says as I zoom out of the parking lot.

"I don't give a fuck!" I shout.

"Of course you don't, you selfish prick!" she screams.

"I'm selfish? That's a joke coming from you."

"How long are you going to hold what I did over my head?"

"Until the day I die."

"I was a teenager. But that's still no excuse for cheating—"

"You're right. It isn't."

"It was a mistake and I've apologized for it!"

"Does that mean you should be freely forgiven?"

"For God's sake, it happened eight years ago!" She throws her arms up.

"Yeah, well, you know the old adage. Once a cheater, always a cheater."

"That's not fair. I'm sorry for how everything went down. It wasn't supposed to happen that way."

"Well, it did."

"You're not innocent in all this. I didn't force you to fuck me."

"You tempted me. I told you to stay away, but you wouldn't listen. I'm not a fucking saint. How long did you expect me to resist your invitation? You might as well have had 'fuck me' tattooed on your forehead."

"If you believe I'm a cheater, then let me go. We're toxic to each other." Her voice wavers. "I can't take this shit anymore."

"I can't let you go!" I punch the steering wheel.

I'm going to make it so there's no mistaking whom she belongs to.

Cin

Art follows behind me with his hands on my hips as I walk up the stairs. The fact that he took me to his penthouse speaks volumes. We're back where we started almost three months ago. He guides me into his bedroom.

"Take off your clothes," he whispers in my ear.

"Are you going to beat me?"

He grasps my chin and turns my head until his mesmerizing green eyes collide with mine. "Don't make me tell you again."

I raise my hand, rubbing my fingertips across his face because I can't help myself. He's a beautiful man.

"Eu te amo," I say.

He closes his eyes as tremors overtake his body. No one will ever experience what we have—love, hate, and unrestrained passion tied together with a bloody red bow. We're constantly on edge. One wrong move and we'll plummet to our deaths, but what a sweet death it'll be.

I wince when he seizes my wrist in a bruising hold.

"Witch," he accuses.

"If I'm a witch, you're a sorcerer."

"If that were true, I'd be able to break the spell you have over me."

"There's no spell. You just don't want to admit the truth."

"Which is?"

"You don't know whether to love or hate me."

"I'm perfectly capable of doing both. I'm a multi-tasker. Now take off your fucking clothes."

Art stands so close to me, the rapid rise and fall of his chest brushes against my back as I undress. His warm breath caresses my neck like the touch of a gentle lover and sends shivers coursing through me. A low moan full of need escapes my mouth when he takes hold of my breasts and circles his thumbs over my nipples until they form hard peaks. His tongue languidly laps at my neck as his hands move down my quivering belly. He plucks and pinches my engorged clit while his other hand descends farther to penetrate my clenching pussy with long fingers. My trembling legs give out. The only thing that stops me from dropping to the floor is Art's hands between my legs. My orgasm is just in reach.

"Eu nunca vou ter o suficiente de você," he says in a tormented voice.

"Nosso destino foi selado no dia em que nos conhecemos. Um não pode ficar sem o outro," I murmur.

He abruptly steps away, causing me to fall to the floor. "You don't get to come."

"Fucking asshole." I glare up at him.

"Someone's grumpy."

"Bite me," I say.

"Get your ass up and go lie in the middle of the bed on your stomach."

I struggle to walk to the bed on shaky legs.

"Hurry the fuck up. I don't have all day."

"I'm going as fast as I can," I snap.

He kicks me in the ass, sending me crashing onto the bed. I throw a pillow at him, but he easily catches it and hits me in the face. Pain explodes in my nose. The soft cotton turns into a dangerous weapon when wielded with force.

"Ouch!"

"Well you started it." He raises the pillow, preparing to strike again.

"Wait!" I say, wrapping my arms around my head.

"I suggest you do what you were told."

"Okay." I hurriedly crawl to the center of the bed.

Once I'm in place, Art cuffs my wrist and ankles. "I'll be back," he says.

"What? Where are you going?"

He doesn't answer me.

"You can't leave me like this."

"I'll be back soon and I'll have a special surprise for you."

"Don't leave me like this! Uncuff me!"

"No can do."

"I'm going to bite your dick off."

He roars with laughter. "Damn, babe, that's violent. I'm rubbing off on you."

"This isn't funny!"

He blows me a kiss before crossing through the doorway. I swear to God I'm going to kill him.

"How's sleeping beauty?"

My eyes open to a smiling Art peering down at me.

Darkness greets me beyond the window. The sun was still out when I fell asleep.

"I can't believe you left me like this for hours!" I shout, seething inside.

"Calm down. You aren't dead."

"What time is it?"

"Nine."

"My mom must be worried sick."

"I sent her a text."

"She probably thinks you murdered me."

"I sent it from your phone."

"You know my passcode?"

"Yep."

"You can't just pry your way into every aspect of my life."

"Sure I can."

God, he's so infuriating.

"I have to pee."

"Too bad."

"My bladder is about to burst."

"I'll get a cup."

"Excuse me? I'm not peeing in a cup!"

"Then pee on yourself."

My blood is boiling. "Fine."

He leaves the bedroom and actually returns with a damn cup. I can't believe him!

"Okay, are you ready?"

I have just enough slack to lift up a little. Once I'm done relieving myself, he puts the cup on the nightstand.

"Can you at least wipe me?"

"It'll air dry." He swats me on the ass.

He better sleep with one eye open after this.

"Are you ready for your surprise?" he asks ominously.

A sense of foreboding washes over me at his tone. Whatever he has planned can't be good.

"During my destructive years, after you ripped my heart out and stomped all over it, I became a tattoo artist for a while." He picks a bag up from the floor.

"What's in there?"

"Everything I need to give you a tattoo."

"Art, you're taking this too fucking far!"

"Trust me, this is nothing compared to what I could do." He pulls items from the bag and positions them across the bed in a straight line.

I thrash against the handcuffs, attempting to get my hands free.

"I'm about to start, so you better stop moving. It'll be your fault if I fuck up."

He puts on a pair of black gloves, then sprays antiseptic on my left butt cheek before wiping the area with a napkin. Next, he draws something on my ass with a sharpie. From this angle I can't tell what it is. I go perfectly still when I hear the buzzing sound. I don't want to end up with a black blob on my ass.

I cringe in pain as he moves the tattoo gun along my skin. "That hurts."

"Stop being a baby. This isn't your first tattoo."

"Well, it's more painful this time."

"I'm almost done."

"What is it?"

"You'll see."

After twenty minutes, I'm on the verge of hysterics wondering what new ink Art is giving me.

"There. It's even better than I imagined." He puts all the materials back in the bag and takes off the gloves before snapping a picture of the tattoo with his cell phone and showing it to me.

Property of Arthur King

"I can't believe you tattooed your name on my ass!" I yell.

"Well it's the truth. It is my ass." He chuckles, uncuffing me from the bed posts.

Once free, I attack him. We roll across the bed and fall onto the floor.

He quickly subdues me. "When are you going to learn that fighting me gets you fucked?"

He grabs me by the throat and jerks me to my feet before throwing me into the window and pinning my body against the glass. "Place your hands flat on the fucking window and keep them there."

"Fuck you!" I scream, refusing to follow his demand.

He slams my face into the glass. Pain erupts in my head as blood seeps from my mouth.

"Now be a good girl and do what you're told."

I comply, realizing he'll always have the upper hand between us.

"I love seeing you bleed." He licks my cheek. "Be defiant again so I can make you bleed some more." He kicks my feet apart.

The sound of his zipper fills my ears.

"What are you thinking right now as my dick opens you up?" he asks, slowly penetrating me.

The exquisiteness of this moment will be burned in my memories forever.

"Tell me," he murmurs.

"I'm afraid."

"Why?"

"You take a little piece of my soul every time you enter my body. Eventually you'll leave me soulless. But what really scares me is that I prefer to be soulless over being without you."

"Welcome to my world." He fully impales me but stays still.

"Please, fuck me," I say in desperation.

"Not yet."

His hardness throbs inside me.

"You feel that?" He covers my hands with his.

I nod, moaning.

"Don't think for one second you can recreate what we have with another man. It can never be done," he says as he begins pumping his hips.

The rolling waves of the ocean model my current emotions. No word in existence is capable of describing the intensity he brings to life inside me. This man could wreck me, hurt me, leave me for dead, but I'll always come back to him because I'd rather stay in hell with the devil than live the rest of my life in paradise. How fucked up is that?

He grinds and rotates his hips wildly as he kisses my neck. Energy builds in my core until I'm completely consumed. My pussy spasms down on his dick as I reach orgasm.

"Você me intoxica," he groans, overfilling my cunt with his semen.

Another piece of my soul is gone, but I don't give a fuck. Art drops to his knees and rests his head against my lower back.

"Why am I so weak when it comes to you?" he asks in a confused voice, more to himself than to me.

Some people are meant to pass through your life while others are destined to stay. Art and I, we're fated to be together. There's nothing I could've done to avoid him. This is meant to be. I am his property.

Cin

My cell phone rings as I pull into a parking space at work. By the time Art took me home last night, my car had already been delivered.

"Hello."

"The video of Art punching that guy is all over the internet!" Anneli exclaims.

"Oh no."

"It's going to be on the gossip news show *What's Poppin?* tonight.

"This is a nightmare."

"What the fuck happened?"

"Art saw us walking together."

"That's it?"

"And we were talking."

"So what? Is that why the fight started?"

"Yeah."

"Are you not allowed to talk to other men?"

"It's a stipulation of our agreement."

"That's absurd!"

"Try telling Art that."

"Are you at work?"

"I just got here. I'm totally going to get fired."

"Maybe not. You can't control the actions of another person."

"But it never would've happened if it wasn't for me."

"Denise is an understanding person. Don't worry."

"I'll talk to you later. It's time to face the music."

"It'll be okay."

I end the call, hoping Anneli is right.

My eyes roam over my surroundings. "Is it me or does this parking lot seem more crowded than it usually is?" I ask myself.

I take a deep breath before getting out of the car. My colleagues give me the side-eye, and students whisper as I walk towards the school. I'm transported back to Central High again—a memory that instantly increases my trepidation. The principal is waiting by my classroom.

"Good morning, Principal Joyner."

"Ms. Belo," she greets. "I would like to have a word with you in my office."

"Absolutely." Here we go.

I enter the office behind her and take a seat in front of the desk.

"I'm sure you're not clueless as to what the topic of discussion will be."

I clear my throat. "I truly apologize for the incident that occurred yesterday. It's inexcusable. I'm devastated it was witnessed by students."

"Are you aware Mr. Skinner is currently in the hospital with a concussion? He also received several stitches to close a gash at the back of his head."

"No."

I went straight to sleep when I got in last night without a thought to calling Jerry to check on him. Guilt and my sore ass make it impossible to sit still.

"Right now, we're not supervisor and employee. I'm a woman speaking candidly to another."

"All right."

"You're a fool for choosing him over Adrian."

If this bitch wants to take it there, that's fine by me. "My personal life is none of your fucking business."

"It became my business when you brought your bullshit on school grounds."

"I assure you there won't be a recurrence."

"You're one of those stupid women who prefer a bad boy over a good man. Your employment is terminated effective immediately."

159

"Then this discussion is over. I'll leave right away."

After Adrian and I stopped dating, her attitude shifted towards me, but it didn't bother me because she remained professional. Well, I guess that's over now. Goddamn it. How will I explain this to my mom?

Art and I are destined to destroy each other's lives.

ART

The music blasting through my ears as I complete overhead presses is interrupted by the ringing of my cell phone. I sit up, pulling the hand towel from around my neck to wipe my sweaty face, and pick my phone up from the floor. Josh's name flashes across the screen. Instead of declining the call, which is my first instinct, I answer knowing exactly why he's calling.

"Yeah."

"Have you watched TV this morning?"

"I have not."

"You're in a heap of trouble."

"I'm shaking in my boots."

"The video clip of you punching that guy is showing everywhere. By now, he knows who you are. A lawsuit is coming for sure."

"I don't give a damn."

"I knew Cin would cause trouble."

"Keep her name out of your fucking mouth."

"You've stayed out of the public's eye since being awarded custody of Mason, but you're back to making the same mistakes because of her."

"Shut the fuck up!"

"She makes you batshit crazy!"

"I need her."

"She brings out the worst in you!"

"I don't care!" I shout.

"She makes you so damn weak."

"I know that, goddamn it!"

"Why can't you just leave her the fuck alone? Jesus, Art. Mason should come first, not her."

"Of course he comes first. But Cin is in my life for good. Accept it."

"It seems to me that your dick comes first."

"I'm done with this topic."

"Have you forgiven her?"

"No, I haven't."

"But still you refuse to let her go."

I look at my cell phone when I hear a beep. Great, it's the old man. "I have to go." I click over. "What do you want?"

"Arthur, are you trying to ruin your life again?"

"I want you and Josh off my case. She's mine, so get used to it."

"I will not have you making a mockery of this family!"

"Oh, you don't need me for that. You accomplish it all on your own."

"You ingrate—"

"Focus on your own life old man." I end the call.

He immediately calls back, but I press decline.

The ringing starts again. He's a persistent bastard, and he's sorely testing my fucking patience. "Give it a fucking rest!" I answer, shouting into the phone.

"Are you fucking kidding me? I should be the one pissed! I just got terminated because of you!" Cin yells.

"It's not the end of the world."

"I want an advance on the money you owe me."

"No."

"No? How is my family supposed to survive?"

"I'll pay all your bills and give you money when you need it."

"Do you know how difficult it'll be to find another teaching position a quarter into the school year?

"It's not a big deal. I'll take care of you."

"You just don't get it. You can't take care of me forever. Sitting home and doing nothing all day isn't for me. I love teaching. The video floating around isn't going to help in my job search."

"It wouldn't have happened if you followed the rules."

"No, it happened because you're a crazed Neanderthal."

"I'll give you a job."

"What?"

"You can be my assistant."

"Don't you already have one?"

"I'll fire her."

"I'm not going to be the reason some poor woman loses her job."

"I'll give her a decent severance package, so she'll be good for a few years."

"I don't want to work for you. I want to teach."

"Trust me, you'll be teaching again by next school year. In the meantime, work for me."

"Working for you would be a conflict of interest."

"Stop making this more complicated than it has to be."

"Do you agree to keep things strictly professional at work?"

"Hell no. If I call you into my office for some midday pussy, I expect you to bend over my desk and spread your legs without question."

"You're ridiculous."

"Do you accept the job or not?"

"Yes."

"Good. I'll pick you up at nine."

"Fine."

"And, Cin?"

"Yes."

"Don't wear any panties."

I end the call before she can respond, and I dial Logan.

"I'm on it. I'll make this disappear. Charges won't be filed and Jerry Skinner will be offered financial compensation for his troubles," he says right away, already deducing the nature of my call.

"Excellent. Let me know when it's done."

"Will do."

I could kick myself for being so excited about seeing Cin every day.

Cin

My mom turns off the television and gets up from the sofa when I enter the apartment, concern evident on her face.

"Cin, I want you to tell me what's going on, and I want to know right this second."

"I got fired today," I say, closing the door.

"Art is more than just a friend, isn't he?"

"Yes." I walk over to the table and sit down.

She stands in front of me with her arms crossed over her chest.

"Mom, I'm sorry I lied to you. Art could never be just a friend to me. I love him."

"Does he love you?"

"We're trying to figure everything out."

"He still thinks you told his secret."

"It's complicated."

"He's not a good man for Sebastian to be around. He's violent and unpredictable. Adrian was good for you."

"Art has always shown kindness towards Sebastian. Do you honestly think I would let him come near my son if he didn't?"

"I didn't mean it like that. I only want the best for you."

"You have to let me live my life. If being with Art is a mistake, it'll be a lesson I'll have to learn on my own."

"I was there to pick up the pieces the last time, remember? You cried almost every night for months. I never want to see you that way again."

"He's my Romeo. It'll always be him."

"There was no happily ever after for them. That love story ended in tragedy."

Art and I were only supposed to be temporary. We were fooling ourselves to think six months would be enough when a lifetime wouldn't be sufficient.

"He can only bring you heartache. When it ends, I'll be there to pick up the pieces again."

I'll break with him, but without him, I'll shatter. Either way I'm fucked, so I might as well stay with Art in purgatory.

"Be quiet, the story about you and Art is up next," Anneli says, stuffing popcorn into her mouth.

We lounge next to each other on her bed. She insisted I come over to watch *What's Poppin*? I've seen it a few times before but decided it wasn't for me. The gossipmongers on the show call themselves "The Posse." There are four of them—Dylan, Mickey, Candy, and Shelly. In my opinion, they're a miserable group who glorify in digging up every dirty detail about the lives of celebrities to discuss on the show.

"This isn't my movie premiere that's going to turn me into an instant sensation overnight, you know."

"Yes, it is. That reminds me, I want your autograph before you leave."

I roll my eyes. "Not hardly."

My eyes are glued to the television, bracing for the bullshit that'll be said about Art and me.

"Arthur King has been out of the spotlight for some time, but yesterday evening he made a grand reappearance. Let's take a look," Dylan says.

The video of Art knocking Jerry out is shown.

"Wow, that was some punch. He could give Mike Tyson a run for his money," Mickey says.

"Do we know what happened?" Dylan asks.

"Apparently, he went into a blind rage because another man was talking to his girlfriend." Shelly wags her eyebrows.

"You're kidding me. Arthur King has a girlfriend? I don't believe it," Candy says.

"It's true. Her name is Cinnamon Belo," Mickey says.

"It won't last. There's no way he'll stay monogamous. The man is a sex machine," Shelly chimes in.

"Ewww, she's dressed like a homeless person." Candy laughs.

"Bitch." I throw popcorn at the television.

"What the hell does he see in her? He could do so much better," Candy adds.

Anneli moves the bowl out of my reach when I go to grab for more. "No wasting delicious snacks here."

"These two have a history. We're going to have a virtual chat with a few of their friends from high school after this commercial break," Dylan says.

"Oh no." I have a sinking feeling one of those friends may be Trevor.

"Who do you think it is?" Anneli asks.

"I'm afraid to find out."

The show comes back on and there on the wall behind "The Posse" is a large screen with Bri and Danny on it.

"We have with us Brianna Lockhart and Danny Livingston to provide some insight about the explosive history between Arthur King and Cinnamon Belo," *Dylan announces.*

"What can you tell us about Art's mystery girl?" *Shelly asks.*

Bri scoffs. "She's hardly a mystery. She's a huge-time slut who cheated on her boyfriend with Art. She became pregnant and didn't know which one was her baby daddy."

"I can't believe we were ever friends with that bitch," Anneli says.

"She's not lying," I say.

I can't be mad at the truth.

"What are your thoughts, Danny?" Candy asks.

"Art has always been a loose cannon—fighting and doing dangerous stunts. Not to mention he tried to kill himself…"

Bri, Danny, and those "Posse" assholes air our dirty laundry for all to see. I'll be considered the biggest slut in the United States, and Art a sick whack job.

"Change the channel. I can't listen to any more of this."

Anneli mutes the television. "Don't let what they're saying get to you."

"It's impossible not to. One day, Sebastian is going to see this interview. What will he think of me?"

"He will think you're an amazing mom who took very good care of him," Anneli says, putting the bowl on the bed to give me a hug.

"I hope you're right."

"I know I am."

"Thank you."

"No problem, babe. How about we find a movie to watch starring hunky Jason Momoa?"

"Sounds good to me." I turn on my back, causing the bowl of popcorn to topple over on the bed.

"Damn, you've been fidgeting since you got on this bed. What's the matter?" Anneli says, cleaning up the mess I made.

"Nothing," I say, looking away from her.

She gives me the side-eye. "You're definitely lying. Tell me what you're hiding. I'll hound you until you do."

"Nothing major. I got new ink."

"What? Why didn't you tell me?"

"It's not a big deal."

"Let me see it."

"It's in a private area."

"Really? I've seen your naked ass plenty of times before. Now strip."

"Okay, but you have to promise not to overreact."

"What the hell did you do?"

I move to my knees, pulling down my bottoms and panties.

"What on earth possessed you to get his name tattooed on your ass?" she shouts.

"It wasn't exactly my choice," I say, tugging my clothes up.

"What do you mean?"

"Art gave me the tattoo."

Her eyes narrow. "Did he force you to do this?"

"We have a unique relationship."

"Answer the question." She looks about ready to kill someone.

"I don't want to."

"You're crazy to have anything to do with him!"

"What Art and I have isn't meant for other people to understand."

"You can't—"

A knock sounds at the door, interrupting her tirade.

"Are you expecting someone?"

"Christian brought dinner."

"I'm going to go. I don't want to be a third wheel."

"Nonsense. I told him you'd be here and he offered to bring enough food for you."

"That was nice of him." I follow Anneli out of the bedroom.

The smile slips from my face when Adrian walks in behind Christian. We haven't seen each other since the day I broke it off with him.

Christian holds up a few pizza boxes. "Dinner is served."

"Yummy. You can put those bad boys right there." Anneli points at the small round table next to the kitchen.

"Sure thing." He kisses her on the cheek. "Hi, Cin, it's nice to see you again."

"Yeah, it's been awhile."

"I'll be right back," Anneli says, closing the door. "I have to use the bathroom."

Adrian and I stare at each other.

"Cat got your tongue?" he jokes.

"Oh, I'm sorry. How have you been?"

"Good, hanging in there. You?"

"The same." There's an awkward pause. "I really should get going. My mom had surgery a few months ago. She's recovering nicely, but I don't want to leave her with Sebastian too long. He can be a handful."

"Don't do that."

"Do what?"

"Use that as an excuse to hightail it out of here."

"I'm—"

"Don't lie."

"I just don't think it's a good idea for me to stay."

"I came here to see you. Christian mentioned you'd be here, so I invited myself. How pathetic is that?"

"Adrian—"

"We had a good thing going, didn't we?" He caresses my jaw. "What went wrong?"

"I'm with Art now."

"Being with someone didn't stop you before."

"I was young and dumb. Don't throw that in my face."

"I'm sorry. I'm still pissed about the whole situation. Why did you choose him over me? I'm good for you, Cin. It's not too late for us."

"There was no chance for us once he came back into my life."

He pulls me close to him and molds his lips to mine.

I break away. "Adrian, stop."

"I still want you, Cin."

"What's going on?" Anneli asks.

"I have to go. I'll call you when I get home, okay?" I leave the apartment.

Today's events have left me drained. I turn off the ignition and exit my car, determined to get inside, take a hot bath, and go to sleep. The headlights of the car parked behind mine flick on. I hold my hand up to shield my eyes. A man steps out of the vehicle, but due to the blinding light, I can only make out his silhouette.

"What the fuck, asshole?"

As the lone figure approaches, I'm able to make out his facial features.

"I've been calling you!" Art shouts.

"I was at Anneli's and forgot my cell in the car."

"What kind of fool do you take me for? You were out fucking another man!"

"That's not true. I was at Anneli's. Call and ask her if you don't believe me!" I yell.

"I can't trust her word. You whores stick together!" he roars.

Art grasps my shoulders and shakes me violently. I bite down on his chin. He retaliates by digging sharp nails into my neck and hauling me to his car. I'm thrown into the back seat, but he doesn't climb in behind me. Instead he gets on his knees on the ground and rips my shoes from my feet.

"What are you doing?" I kick out at him.

"I'm going to smell your pussy, and if it smells like sex, I swear to God I'll beat the living shit out of you."

He yanks my jeans down my legs and throws them to the ground.

"I told you where I was."

He punches my leg. "Stop fucking kicking me!"

"Ouch!"

Next, my panties are torn from my body and my legs forced apart. He buries his face between my legs and inhales deeply.

"The loveliest aroma I've ever had the pleasure of smelling," he growls before sliding his tongue over my clit.

"Art," I moan, closing my thighs over his head as he laps at my pussy.

He gorges on my cunt, the ferocity of his feasting obliterating my cognitive abilities. I whimper in frustration when he lifts his head.

"Should I let you come?"

"Yes."

"But you've been a bad girl."

"I'm sorry."

"You better make sure your cell phone stays by your side because if this happens again, you won't be able to sit for a fucking month."

"I understand. Please…" I beg.

His warm mouth latches onto my clit, and I come within minutes. Once the shudders subside, he crawls up my body, peering into my eyes while he slowly sinks his dick inside my saturated cunt. My passion-filled moans are swallowed by his kisses. I wrap my legs around him and cross my ankles at his lower back as he bulldozes through my center, showing me no mercy. My pending orgasm ebbs, then flows, until it breaks free. Art's gyrating hips increase the magnitude of my climax tenfold, creating a perfect storm of ecstasy.

"Oh fuck," he grunts, attaining his end.

We hold on to each other, basking in the afterglow of completion.

"Remember what I said," he says between breaths. "I will hurt you if you don't listen."

"You hurt me even when I do."

"I can't help it."

"I know."

Can love between a man and woman be too strong? Maybe a love like this is destined to end in tragedy.

Cin

It really sucks being fired from a position I loved, but I have to admit it felt really good being able to cook breakfast for Sebastian and walk him to the bus stop. At nine o'clock sharp, Art sends me a text.

"Okay, Mom. I have to go." I walk to the sofa and bend over to kiss her forehead.

"What are your job responsibilities?"

She's not happy about my unpredictable relationship with Art—if I can even call it that. I don't know what we are, but I can't go on pretending he's not important to me. Being without him isn't an option.

"I'm not sure. Assisting."

"Cinnamon."

"Mom, don't worry."

"Why you shouldn't be together is what draws you to each other. I understand what you're feeling. I really do. I was young once. The exhilaration of going headfirst into a pitch-black room hoping to find a ray of light will lose its appeal. Trust me, the excitement eventually fades. Baby, what you have with him isn't love. It's lust."

"I couldn't turn my back on him even if I wanted to. Everything in my heart rebels at the thought of it."

"How can I dissuade you from this path?"

"There's nothing you can do, Mom." My cell phone rings. "I have to go. Call me if you need anything. I love you."

"I love you too," she says, resigned.

Art is waiting in another one of his expensive cars as I emerge from the building.

How many does he have?

"Hey," I say, getting into the car.

"How'd you sleep?"

"Good. You?"

"After that orgasm, I slept like a baby. I hope you're panty-less today."

"I am."

"Good. You're finally following directions." He drives out of the parking lot and maneuvers into the flow of traffic.

"Did you watch *What's Poppin* yesterday?"

"I don't watch bullshit like that."

"Bri and—"

"Cin, I don't give a fuck. I've been in the limelight long enough to learn to ignore shit like that. You need to be prepared."

"For what?"

"You've been branded as my girlfriend."

"Am I?"

He continues as if I hadn't asked the question. "You'll start noticing people gawking at you, whispering, pointing, and taking pictures. The paparazzi may even start following you."

He laughs at my horrified expression.

"You'll get used to it. Don't let it bother you."

"That's easy for you to say."

"Soon it'll become a normal part of your day."

"If you say so."

"When was the last time you saw Adrian?"

There's no way he could possibly know I saw him last night.

"Where did that question come from?" I ask, not meeting his gaze.

"Don't fucking play with me. Answer the damn question."

"I haven't seen Adrian since the day I ended it with him." I shouldn't have lied, but he'll blow my seeing Adrian last night way out of proportion.

"Are you lying to me?"

"No."

"Look at me."

Unwillingly, I turn to face him.

"Are. You. Lying. To. Me?"

"I saw him last night," I blurt.

His knuckles turn white as his hands tighten on the steering wheel. "Did you fuck him?"

"No, I swear. He came to Anneli's apartment with her boyfriend, but I left right away."

"Did he touch you?"

"Art—"

"Answer me!" he booms.

"He kissed me."

He punches the dashboard. "Did you kiss him back?"

I shake my head.

"Did you like it?"

"No, I only want you."

"What did you do when he kissed you?"

"I pushed him away."

Art is a lot calmer than I thought he'd be upon hearing this, which scares me.

"He'll be dealt with later."

"Please don't do anything stupid."

"You'll be dealt with too, for lying to me."

"I was afraid of your reaction."

"Now you can be afraid of the consequences."

"I had no idea he was going to be there."

"I'll choke the life out of you before I let another man have you and damn us both."

ART

Her face turns pale at my harsh words, but she needs to understand if she keeps fucking with me there'll be dire consequences. I pull into the driveway of a large house.

"Where are we?"

"Come on." I get out of the car.

Once we're inside, I watch Cin take in the spacious living room.

"I just closed on this place."

"What are you going to use it for?"

"I bought it for you."

Her head whips in my direction. "I can't accept this."

"You have thirty days to vacate your apartment."

"I'm not putting in a notice."

"That's fine. One was already put in on your behalf."

"You must've paid a fortune for this house."

"The price wasn't a factor in my decision to purchase. It's good for Sebastian. He'll have his own room, a big backyard with a swimming pool, and it's only a block from his school. You want the best for him. I'll make sure he'll have it."

She stares at me, trying to decipher the truth of my words.

"Your mother will have a room as well and there's a two-car garage, so when she gets a vehicle there'll be space for it. Do you want a tour?"

"Yeah."

"As you can see, it's fully furnished."

"Who chose all this stuff?"

"I did, with the assistance of an interior decorator. I'll replace whatever you don't like."

"It's all wonderful, and I'm not picky about this sort of stuff anyway."

Cin's eyes and smile grows wider with each room we visit. She throws her arms around my neck.

"Thank you so much for this! My mom and Sebastian will be so excited!" She releases me and darts down the hall to the master bedroom.

Seeing her happy like this pulls at my heart.

"This is all yours," I say, entering the bedroom.

No expense was spared for her. All the furniture is white marble.

"Do you really think I need a vanity?" She laughs.

"The decorator assured me a vanity is a must-have for all women." I smirk.

"But I'm not like other women."

"No, you're not."

I pick her up and throw her onto the bed. The alarm on her face hardens my dick.

"Get naked and turn on your belly." I unbuckle my leather belt and pull it off.

"Why?" Her eyes warily track my movements.

"It's time for your punishment."

"No."

She rolls over and attempts to crawl to the other side of the bed, but I grab her ankle and pull her back. I jump on the bed and sit on her back, facing her pretty ass. She flails her arms and legs, but we know her efforts are fruitless, there's no way she's strong enough to unseat me.

"You're too heavy. I can't breathe," she pants.

"Stop fighting and it'll be over quick."

"What about my tattoo? It's still healing!"

"Too bad." I expose her bottom.

"Art, you can't treat me like a fucking child!" She bucks beneath me.

"Take your punishment like a woman." I whip my arm through the air and strike her as hard as I can.

"You fucking asshole! I hate you!"

Cin damns me to hell and calls me every expletive in the English language. I'm satisfied when the skin of her inflamed ass glows a bright red. I fling the belt to the floor, then move to her side. She sits up, shredding my skin with her sharp nails. She screams in fury as I rip her shirt from her body. Her teeth latch onto my forearm, biting down hard. I seize her jaw and squeeze to pry her away.

"Oh, you want to play rough." I snatch off her shoes.

"Motherfucker!" She begins pounding her fists on my chest.

I push her back down and pull her jeans off.

"No!" she yells.

"Yes," I counter, forcing her legs apart.

She socks me in the face. I grab her wrists, pinning them above her head with one hand, and free my engorged dick with the other. I ram home, not caring if I cause her pain. Cin's fiery hot sheath just might reduce my dick to ashes. Fuck, her cunt grips my dick in a vise-like hold.

"Do you want me to stop?"

"Yes."

"Then why is your pussy so wet?" I nuzzle her neck.

I tunnel through her walls seeking release. Our moans reverberate around the bedroom. She writhes and bucks under me, clamping her pussy muscles down on my dick, causing me to lose my shit. I swiftly move my hips between her thighs, hitting her cervix with each punishing stroke as my balls slap against her ass. *Her sex is perfection personified.* Adrenaline flows through my veins, heightening my senses. Her inner muscles flex as her shattered cry fills my ears. I erupt, pounding into her until there's nothing left, and I collapse. Then something amazing happens I've never experienced before. Her pussy flutters over my still-hard length and I come again.

"Holy fuck," I groan. I'm so weak I can't move. After my breathing steadies, I find the strength to roll to my back.

"How can you hurt me like that?"

"If you're expecting me to feel remorse for what I did, you'll be disappointed."

"Because of you, I have a sore pussy and ass."

"Next time, you'll think twice about lying. I'm hoping you don't, because I do so love to abuse your delectable body."

"You don't walk away unscathed." She looks pointedly at the teeth marks on my forearm.

"Oh, that's nothing." I shrug. "I barely felt it."

"Well, the next time I'll be sure to take a great big chunk out of you."

"See, you're already thinking negatively. You must be planning on breaking the rules again."

"One day I'll get the best of you."

I laugh. Damn, I admire her spirit. "You can try. Get in the shower. We have to go."

"What exactly will I be wearing since you destroyed my shirt and bra?" she deadpans.

"Go look in the closet."

She dramatically inches off the bed.

I laugh at her antics. "It looks like you're in critical condition. Maybe we should stop by the hospital."

"Kiss my ass." She walks towards the closet, rubbing her red behind.

"Bring it back over here and I'll lick it too."

"There's no way I'll be able to sit down today without a bag of ice taped to my ass," she says, opening the closet door. "Oh my God."

"Do you like what you see?"

She looks at me with eyes large as saucers. "This closet is the same size as my apartment."

"Go inside and explore."

"I'm assuming you didn't choose these clothes yourself," she calls out to me.

"Nope, I hired a stylist."

She comes out with a white G-string hanging from the tip of her index finger. "There's a drawer full of these. I wonder why." She arches an eyebrow.

"Well, knowing how much you like them, I made sure you had at least five hundred pairs." I offer her a Cheshire smile.

"Five hundred?"

"I overexaggerated a little. It's actually four hundred and ninety-eight pairs," I joke.

She chuckles. "You're cute when you're like this."

My mood changes instantly. She makes me forget her deceit so easily. Alarm registers on her face when I leap from the bed and converge on her.

I push her, causing her to fall onto the settee in the middle of the closet. "Get dressed and be downstairs in ten minutes."

"No, I'm taking a shower first," she says, glaring at me in defiance.

"Are you ready for another battle so soon, little girl?" I walk up to her and reach my hand behind her to run my fingertips along her bruised ass. "You barely survived this one."

"You confuse me, Art." She places a soft kiss on my neck. "I'm tired of the cat-and-mouse game between us, aren't you?" Her russet-colored eyes search mine, expecting to find something that isn't there.

"No, I live for the game. The question you have to ask yourself this very moment is—are you ready to play again?"

Her eyes narrow. "I'm up for a second round."

I grab her hair and violently jerk her head back. "I was hoping you'd say that."

I blink in surprise when she slaps me across the face.

"Bravo. One point for Cin." I swing her around, sliding my arm over her slender neck.

I lead her to the row of colorful dresses. "Which do you prefer to wear? I'm partial to the blue one."

"I don't want to wear a damn dress."

"I rarely see you in one, so today you're wearing a dress whether you like it or not."

Not happy with my response, she reaches up, grabs two fistfuls of my hair, and yanks me forward.

I apply more pressure to her throat. "Be a good girl and let go."

She accepts defeat and drops her arms to her sides after a few minutes of struggling to gain freedom.

"Which one, sweetheart? We really do have to get going," I say sweetly, as if we're a normal couple heading out to Sunday brunch with friends.

"The purple," she grits out.

I pull the blue dress from the hanger. "You can wear the purple one tomorrow. Are you going to dress yourself, or will I have to do it?"

"I'll do it," she snaps.

I dangle the dress in front of her. "Here you go."

She snatches it from my grasp. "You can let me go now."

"Victory is mine," I say, heading towards the bedroom. Before clearing the doorway, I glance over my shoulder. "And, Cin?"

"What?" Her eyes shoot daggers at me.

"No panties." I wink at her, just to piss her off more. "How about round three later if you're feeling lucky?"

She picks up a shoe from the rack housing dozens of pairs and throws it at me. I quickly dart out of the closet. When Cin starts to get under my skin, stirring emotions best left dormant, I tip the scale, upsetting the balance and pulling us further from the peace we could have together. I want to trust her again, but my pride stops me.

Cin

What an eventful morning. My head has yet to stop spinning from the unexpected turn of events. Art bought me a fucking house. My reservations evaporated once he pointed out the benefits for Sebastian. For the first time he'll have his own bedroom, and God knows I'm beyond thrilled at the prospect of privacy. After leaving the house, we went to a business meeting at the headquarters of a construction company. Art plopped a laptop in front of me and instructed me to take minutes. I tried my best to be thorough, but the notes are terrible. Being an assistant is obviously not my forte. It wasn't hard to decipher I didn't belong among the attendees. To make matters worse I couldn't stop squirming because of my sore ass. The pain along with sticky thighs was a reminder of our fucking an hour before, making it difficult to concentrate. The meeting was long and boring, but it was interesting to learn Art plans to build a few more Falcon locations in Florida. The executives put on a good show, driving home the pros of Art selecting their company for the upcoming projects. Thankfully, after several excruciating hours, the meeting finally ended. Art gave me a few action items to complete as we left the building.

Now we're at a fancy Japanese restaurant. I'm out of my element here too, having never eaten this type of food, so Art decided for me. He ordered the food in Japanese, so I have no idea what's in store. He tried to coerce me into trying caviar, but I vehemently refused.

"Woman, stop fidgeting," Art barks from across the table.

"I'm certainly not doing it for my own enjoyment," I snap.

"Using that tone of voice with me will get you another spanking."

"Jackass," I mumble under my breath.

"What's that?"

"Oh nothing," I say, fluttering my eyelashes and rubbing my chin with my middle finger.

He notices my gesture. "Cute."

The waiter comes by the table to deliver a platter and top off our wine glasses. My nose wrinkles at the contents on the plate.

"What the hell? This isn't enough food for a toddler."

"This is what you call fine dining."

"Well, I call it a rip-off. What is it anyway?"

"Sashimi."

"Which is?"

"Thinly sliced raw meat."

I make a gagging sound. "I'm definitely not eating that."

"What we have here is Wagyu beef, tuna, cuttlefish, and sea bream."

"I'll pass."

"You need to get out of your comfort zone. Put some grated ginger and garlic on it, then dip it in the soy or *ponzu*. If you want a little heat, you slather some wasabi paste on it."

I put on my big girl panties and pick up the chopsticks.

"How do I use these things?"

"First of all, you're holding them incorrectly." He chuckles. "Watch me."

I follow his lead, managing to pick up a piece of fish and successfully dip it in soy sauce.

"If I barf all over the table, it'll be your fault," I warn before popping the meat in my mouth. "Wow, it's actually pretty tasty." Maybe working for Art won't be so bad. I'm making a decent salary and having a delicious lunch thrown in is a great perk. What more could a girl ask for?

"See, listen to me and you'll experience great things."

"I wouldn't go that far."

"Hello, Art, I thought that was you."

I glance towards the vaguely familiar voice. Oh no, it's the guy from the fundraiser dinner. He takes a chair from the empty table next to us and deposits it beside me before sitting.

"Leonard," Art says scathingly.

"Cinnamon, it's a pleasure seeing you again." He reaches for my hand, but Art grabs his wrist and flings his arm back.

"Please, behave like adults. I prefer not to be featured on *What's Poppin?* again," I say in irritation.

"It's not a crime to say hello to a friend, is it?" Leonard asks.

"You know what you're doing," I accuse.

"I'm here alone and was wondering if I could join you two for lunch."

"No," Art snaps, drawing the attention of a few patrons.

"Leonard, please go," I beg.

"Since you asked so nicely, I'll be on my way." He stands, watching me with hungry eyes. "I look forward to seeing you around."

"The next time we meet there won't be witnesses," Art threatens.

"I'm scared shitless," Leonard says tauntingly, walking away.

"Has he sampled your pussy yet?"

"I haven't even seen him since the charity dinner," I say, annoyed.

"You better keep it that way. Do you understand me?"

"Yes," I hiss, incensed by his highhanded attitude, but agree to avoid an argument that would draw more attention to us.

We finish lunch in silence, our light mood gone.

"Where to next, boss man?" I ask from the passenger seat.

"Kids That Swim."

"What will I do there?"

"My grant writer could always use additional help."

"Grant writer?"

"She raises funds through private donors, foundations, and government grants."

"I thought you financed everything."

"That wouldn't be a very smart business decision. Sure, I provide a significant amount of my own money, but fully funding the facility isn't financially sound."

"Oh, okay. That makes sense." I obviously have a lot to learn about business and nonprofits.

Once Art parks, we make our way inside the building.

"Good afternoon, Mr. King."

"Madelyn."

"And Cinnamon, it's always a pleasure to see you."

"Likewise," I say, following Art up the stairs.

We stop at an office to the left.

He knocks on the door. The beautiful golden-haired woman sitting behind the desk looks up, offering him, in my opinion, a flirtatious smile. When her eyes land on me, the smile disappears. Interesting. Either they're fucking or she has a major crush on him. She comes around the desk as we move farther into the room. Out of the dozen times I've been here, I've never seen her. Granted, I'd only been to the second floor on my first visit.

"I would like for you to meet Cinnamon Belo, my new assistant."

I hold out my hand. "It's nice to meet you."

Her eyes travel the length of my body, sizing me up. "Francesca Levy."

"Cin is available to help with any existing projects."

She pauses for a heartbeat, clearly not liking the idea. "I'm sure I'll be able to find something to keep her occupied."

"Great. If needed I'll be in my office," he says, leaving us.

"Well, I'm all yours. What can I do?"

"Have you ever edited before?"

"No, but it shouldn't be too hard to spot typos."

"We shall see," she says snidely, handing me a binder off the desk.

"Is there a problem?" I ask, itching to knock this uppity bitch down a few pegs.

"Not at all." She gives me a phony confused expression. "Read through this document and make note of any errors you see. There's an empty office across the hall. You can work in there."

I nod, leaving the room.

A couple hours later, I head back to Francesca's office, finished with the task assigned to me.

"Hi, I'm all done," I say, handing her the binder.

"Thank you." She pastes a fake smile on her face. "So, are you and Mr. King together?"

"How is that any of your business?" I snap.

"I saw the video. He would never have behaved that way if it wasn't for you. You're no good for him."

"Oh, are you an expert on what he needs?"

"Of course I am. I've been with him since this facility opened. One day he'll realize we make sense together."

I laugh. "Trust me, you've barely scratched the surface of the enigma that is Art."

"You're a dirty little skank who'll be thrown out on your ass soon enough."

I place my palms on the desk and lean in closer to her. "I'm the woman he'd kill for—the woman he can't let go. I'll never be replaced." I leave, storming towards Art's office.

He has some explaining to do. His door is shut, but I barge in anyway, not giving a damn if he's busy.

He's leaning back in the chair with his cell phone to his ear.

"I need to talk to you." I interrupt him mid-sentence.

"I'll call you back." He ends the call. "What's the problem?"

"Are you fucking her?"

"Who?"

"Francesca! Don't play stupid."

"Stop being ridiculous. I would never fuck an employee."

My eyebrows nearly shoot to my hairline at the declaration.

"Well, you're the exception."

"She wants you."

"Francesca and I have a strictly professional relationship, and that's all it'll ever be."

"She thinks you two are going to be together one day. She even called me a skank."

His expression becomes thunderous.

"Sit," he demands. "I'll be back."

"What are you going to do?"

In a few long strides, he's out of sight.

I plunk down in the chair. Shit, maybe I should've kept my big fat mouth closed. Jealousy got the better of me. She's just so gorgeous and I'm so plain. I feel a little intimidated by her.

He's back a half hour later.

"What happened?"

"I fired her," he says nonchalantly, sitting on the edge of his desk.

"I didn't want to ruin the woman's livelihood for God's sake."

"Calm down. Francesca will hardly be destitute. She's a freelance consultant who comes in twice a week and has dozens of clients. Her services are no longer required."

"Because of me."

"No one is allowed to disrespect you."

"Except you."

"Correct. It's quitting time, let's go."

"Okay, you're the boss."

"Damn straight."

Cin

"Wow, this house is amazing and the furniture is to die for," Anneli gushes, running her fingers along the marble countertop. "This kitchen is a chef's wet dream."

There was no sense in waiting thirty days to move, so we got up early this morning to get things going. I told Mom and Sebastian the news when I got home yesterday evening. Sebastian is over the moon, ecstatic about finally having a bedroom all to himself. My mom, on the other hand, has concerns. She thinks it's a mistake to put our trust in Art, fearing we'll be thrown out on the streets if he becomes angry with me. I explained that's not the type of man Art is. We have our issues—there's no doubt about it—but he'd never see Sebastian homeless. I'd bet my life on it. The move was easy since we only needed to pack our clothes and toiletries. Everything else was provided for, from silverware to appliances. What's left behind will be donated to charity. Mom's trepidation faded a little once she saw our new dwellings. She's excited to have her own space as well. We've spent too many years living in close quarters.

"Mom!" Sebastian yells.

Anneli and I walk into the living room. He runs towards me in a flurry of cheerful delight.

"My bedroom is amazing! I have a PlayStation 4, a Nintendo Switch, and loads of other cool stuff!"

"I'm glad you're satisfied."

"Art is the best ever! You should marry him!"

That comment throws me for a loop.

"He would be an awesome dad for me. Don't you think, Mom?" He peers at me with hopeful eyes.

Anneli makes a clucking sound, giving me a withering look.

"I'm sure he would," I answer.

"You should ask him. And Mason would be my real brother. I've always wanted a brother."

"How about I make us some lunch?" I change the subject. "Go finish exploring your room and I'll call you once it's ready."

"Okay," he says in disappointment.

"I'll help you," Anneli says.

She starts in on me as soon as we enter the kitchen. "Have you considered the repercussions of your actions and what it could mean for Sebastian?"

"Of course I have."

"Does Art have such a hold on you that you'd jeopardize the happiness of your son?"

"I'm doing this for his happiness."

"In the beginning you were, but not now."

"Stay out of my business, Anneli."

"Are you fucking kidding me right now? I'm your best friend. Your business is mine. And it's my job to tell you when you're fucking up big time. You're not thinking clearly."

"I'm not having this conversation." I open the refrigerator and gather lunch meat, cheese, and mayo for sandwiches before moving to the counter.

"This was his plan all along." She walks over to stand beside me.

"What are you talking about?"

"The first step is dependence, which he's accomplished. You depend on him for everything now, which is exactly what he wants. He purposely got you terminated."

"You're being ridiculous. Art isn't a psychic. He couldn't have known Jerry and I would be walking together."

"Why was he at the school? Have you ever asked him?"

What if she's right and my judgment can't be trusted? My love for him could be blinding me, causing me to overlook the glaring signs right in front of my face. The two people whose opinions I value the most disapprove of my relationship, and in truth, I don't blame them. Were the roles reversed, I'd feel the same way.

"No, I haven't, but I can assure you it wasn't for nefarious purposes. He's a possessive jealous man. That's all."

"He wanted a reason to cause trouble for you. Why can't you see that?" she asks in frustration.

"Art wasn't going to hit Jerry until he reached for me."

"Why are you always defending him?" she yells.

"Keep your voice down," I whisper. The last thing I need is for my mom to hear the accusations Anneli's throwing out. She'll become paranoid all over again.

"Your mother needs to hear this."

"She's happy. Don't ruin the day for her."

She grudgingly relents, lowering her voice. "I'm pretty sure Art has an undiagnosed case of bipolar disorder. The man needs professional help. My God, Cin, he permanently marked you. Only a crazy person would do that."

"Art and I may not make sense to other people, but we belong together."

"Please use your brain," she groans.

"I can't. I have to use my heart."

"You both can live a happy life, Cin, but not together. It's hard for you to face the truth because you love him."

"The thought of being without him is unbearable. Losing Art once nearly destroyed me. Losing him again would kill me. We'll never be perfect, and that's okay. I just want him."

"Leave him. We'll get through the aftermath together," she pleads.

"Anneli, you're more than a friend to me. I consider you my sister. But I won't budge on this." She opens her mouth to speak, but I hold up my hand. "Hear me out. I love you, and I'll be forever grateful for your unwavering support throughout the years."

I abandon my task and fully face Anneli. It's important she understands how serious I am and sees the determination in my eyes. I want her to accept that my mind will not be changed by her or anyone else.

"I'm riding with Art until the fucking wheels fall off. Even if we crash and burn, I'm still not getting out. Please don't let my decision come between us."

"I can't tell you how to live your life. But I'll be there with a fire extinguisher to put out the flames and to help you escape if you decide you've had enough."

I throw my arms around her in a tight hug. "Thank you."

"You're welcome, babe."

Though the likelihood of Art and me finding our happy place is slim, I'm not ready to give up.

ART

The scene before me is so damn domestic. Cin prepares breakfast while the boys and I sit at the island bar. They play with action figures to keep themselves entertained until we're served. Cin moves around my kitchen, humming and dancing. The sight is lovely. I doubt she even realizes what she's doing. Cin is passionate about cooking, so she's in her zone. She and Sebastian stayed the night. We still pretend to sleep in separate bedrooms in the best interest of the boys. Her movements cease and a pretty pink blush covers her delicate features when she catches me staring.

"Don't stop on my account."

The doorbell rings. Who the hell could be visiting this early on a Sunday morning? Marisa and Heather—Mason's nanny—are off today.

"I'll be right back," I say, leaving the kitchen.

It has to be Josh or my grandfather. No one else would be bold enough to stop by unannounced. Only three other people have the code to the gate, and one is here with me. There's not a lot of shit on this earth that can shock me, but I'm momentarily speechless by who I find waiting on my doorstep. I never thought I'd lay my eyes on her again. The audacity of this bitch to show herself after being MIA for so long is astounding.

"What the fuck are you doing here?"

"Hi, Art, it's so good to see you," my mother says. "Can I come in?"

She hasn't aged, still beautiful as ever—the perfect Barbie doll. Everything about my mother sickens me, from her perfectly styled hair to her designer clothes, shoes, and accessories.

"How did you get the code to the gate?"

"Your grandfather gave it to me."

Fucking asshole. The code will be changed, and he will not be privy to it. "You are not welcome here."

"Please, I want to see Mason."

"I will never allow you near him."

"You can't keep me from him. I'm his mother and have a right to see him."

"You gave up your parental rights when you abandoned him three years ago."

"I made a terrible—"

"Spare me your goddamn excuses."

"During that time, I was taking anti-depressants, and felt it was best to leave him with you."

"You've failed all of your sons."

"I tried my best to be a good mother."

"If that was you at your best, I'd hate to see you at your worst. You don't have a maternal bone in your body."

"I'll file a petition for visitation."

"My lawyers will bury you in a court battle. Try your hand if you think you have a chance at winning, but understand I'll kill you before I let you hurt him." I slam the door in her face.

Going back to the kitchen is not an option in my current state, so I head to the gym instead. It's my duty to protect them, even from me. They're the most important people in my life.

Cin

Where the hell is he? I went to his office, then the bedroom, but he's nowhere to be found. His breakfast is getting cold. I head towards the gym next. There I find him, beating the shit out of a poor punching bag.

"Art?"

He turns wild eyes on me.

"What's the matter?"

"Go back to the kitchen!" he roars.

"No. Not until you tell me what's wrong. I just want to help." I approach him warily.

Whoever visited earlier pissed him off.

"Leave, goddamn you!"

"No." I hold firm.

He charges me, grips my throat with his powerful hand, and completely lifts me off my feet.

"You push and push when you should quit while you're ahead!" he shouts, hurtling me across the room.

I hit the wall with a thud, causing air to whoosh from my lungs before sliding to the floor. Pain explodes in my right arm, but it doesn't seem to be broken.

"Please talk to me. Hurting me is not going to help you."

"Maybe not, but it feels fucking good."

"You're going to rot from the inside out holding all this hate in your heart. It's not good for you or Mason. Let it go before it's too late," I beg.

The anger drains out of him at my words and is replaced with confusion. He looks so lost. Everything in me demands I comfort him. After clambering to my feet, I move cautiously towards him, testing the limits again. I don't stop until the tip of his nose brushes against my forehead. I'm invading his personal space, hoping he doesn't go on the attack once more. Slowly, I wrap my arms around him. He returns the embrace and squeezes tightly as he buries his face in my neck. I pull back, grasping his hand, and lead him to the exercise bench where we both sit.

He takes a deep breath. "It was my mother at the door."

"What did she want?"

"To spend time with Mason."

"And you don't think it's a good idea."

"Of course not. Do you?"

"I know your mom doesn't have the best track record, but I think you should give her a chance. If Trevor were to show up one day asking to be a part of Sebastian's life, I wouldn't be opposed."

"How could you so easily let him back into your lives?" he asks in anger.

"I owe it to Sebastian to give Trevor every opportunity to be in his life."

"There's no turning back once I agree to this. If she bails, it'll crush him and I'll never be able to forgive myself."

"If she doesn't follow through we'll be right there to offer Mason comfort."

He cups my cheek with the palm of his hand and rests his forehead against mine. "Thank you."

"You're welcome."

ART

That damn Cin can talk me into doing anything. I check my watch again in agitation, then glance at the entrance to the restaurant. My mother was supposed to meet me for lunch at noon, and it's now twelve-fifteen. One thing I'm anal about is punctuality. She's lucky I've waited here this long. I'll give her another five minutes before leaving. I take another sip of wine, getting more irritated by the second. This was a bad idea. My mother is unreliable. Just as I decide to call the whole thing off, she enters the establishment, frantically searching for me. I raise my hand to get her attention. Spotting me, the worried expression on her face is replaced with a smile. She quickly strides to the table and sits across from me.

"I'm so sorry for being late." She wiggles her fingers, showcasing the bright red polish on her nails. "I decided to go to the spa this morning."

"I guess that's more important than meeting me to discuss Mason."

"I'm only fifteen minutes late."

"Twenty."

"I apologized."

"Which doesn't mean shit coming from you."

"I'll never be good enough in your eyes."

"You're right, you won't, but this meeting isn't about you and me. It's too late for us. If you've really changed your selfish ways, I'm willing to allow visitation with Mason."

"You don't know how happy you just made me." She clasps her hands together in excitement.

"How long do you plan to stay in Orlando?"

"I'm meeting with a realtor after lunch to locate a permanent residence. I want to be close to Mason."

My mother's intentions are good, but I don't trust her to keep her word.

"I'm only giving you this opportunity once. If you blow it, that's it. Don't reappear years from now asking for another chance."

"Thank you so much, Art. I'm so thrilled you called me."

"Your thanks are unfounded. If it wasn't for Cin, this meeting would never have happened."

"Oh, I remember hearing of her. Are you two together?"

"Something like that."

"You love her. I can tell."

"Love is a foreign concept to you. You wouldn't know the first thing about it. Anyway, we aren't here to talk about my love life."

"Okay, you're right. When can I see him?"

"You can either wait for the weekend or you can see him tomorrow night."

"Tomorrow is great. I'll take him to dinner."

"No. You can visit with him at my place. If it goes well, then you can take him to dinner Wednesday night."

"Right. I understand the need to ease him into this."

"Be there by seven, on the dot."

"I'll be early. I promise."

I wish I could believe her. "I need you to answer one question."

"Sure."

"Who's his father?"

"It doesn't—"

"Answer the fucking question," I snap. "He deserves to know."

"I only know his first name." She suddenly finds the napkin in front of her interesting, too embarrassed to meet my gaze.

"Excuse me?"

"I met a fellow traveler in Greece, and we had a fling for a day or two. He left without saying goodbye."

"He'll never know who his father is." I sigh.

Mason is probably better off not knowing, but he won't see it that way. He'll always have an empty hole inside him only the presence of a father could fill. I can attest to that firsthand. Though my father was around sometimes, he was never fully there. Not only will this be hard for Mason, but he'll start to wonder if he has siblings out there. Maybe I should try to locate the guy for Mason's sake. It will be damn near impossible though, given it's been almost six years and my mother wasn't even smart enough to ask for the guy's last name.

"I have to go." I stand, pulling a few bills from my wallet and tossing them on the table. "Order whatever you want."

"But you haven't eaten yet. I was hoping we could catch up and talk more."

"You shouldn't have been late then." I stride towards the exit, hoping I made the best decision for my brother.

Mason's attention turns from playing his video game to me when I enter his bedroom.

"Are you winning?" I ask, sitting on the bed beside him.

I came straight to his room after arriving home with the intention of telling him about tomorrow's plan, but now I can't bring myself to do it. I'm afraid of failing him. My childhood was filled with disappointment, and I promised myself his wouldn't be. Growing up my mother never came to football games, offered words of encouragement, or consoled me if I got hurt. She treated me like a Christmas ornament, only acknowledging when absolutely necessary. After she was done showing me off, I would be packed away until needed again. Can a tiger really change its stripes? I look at the picture of our mother on his nightstand, positioned next to one of Cole. Not too long ago he asked for a picture of her. It took a while, but I found one. I have to do this for him, even though it fills me with dread.

"No, I always lose." He pouts.

"It takes practice. You'll get it soon enough." I rub the top of his curly head. "I need to talk to you about something really important."

Being very perceptive for his age, Mason picks up on the serious note in my voice. He lays the joystick on the bed and faces me.

"I saw Mom today."

His eyes light up as he leaps to his feet on the bed and jumps up and down. "My mommy is back! My mommy is back! I knew she would come back for me!" he yells in happiness.

I grab his arm and pat the space next to me. "Sit down, Mason."

He drops to his bottom. I feel his tiny body vibrating with excitement.

"Where is she?"

"She's coming tomorrow, but—"

"I'm going to be a good boy so she'll never leave me again."

"Her leaving had nothing to do with you. Don't ever think you caused her to go. Some people aren't meant to stay in one place."

His large eyes fill with unshed tears. This news is taking an emotional toll on him. "Why didn't she take me with her?" he asks, lips quivering.

"She had to be alone."

"But why?"

"I don't have an answer for you."

"Can you make her stay?" He eyes me expectantly, looking for confirmation I'll ensure his request is met.

"I'm sorry, buddy. I can't make that promise."

"What if she goes away again?"

"You'll still have me."

"What about Cin and Sebastian?"

"They're not going anywhere."

If Cin tries to leave, I'll drag her back—kicking and screaming if I have to.

"Mom is supposed to stop by for a few hours tomorrow." Now here comes the hard part. "Mason," I say, gently. "Can you be a big boy for me?"

"Yes," he says resolutely.

"I need to say this, to prepare you. Okay?"

He nods in understanding. The vulnerability in his eyes is killing me, and I hate I'm the cause of it.

"Sometimes things don't go the way you expect them to. I'm telling you this because there's a chance Mom may not show up tomorrow."

Tears spill down his chubby cheeks. I pull him onto my lap, offering comfort. It had to be said to set the expectation.

ART

Mason insisted we wait outside for our mother to arrive. He watches the gate eagerly while I sit on the top step, leaning back against a pillar, reveling in his excitement. Unfortunately, the jubilance is short lived as more time passes and there's no sign of her. Uneasiness overcomes me, so I send her a text message.

Me: Where the hell are you?

By seven-fifteen, I know she's not coming. Damn Cin for talking me into giving that bitch a chance. I should've listened to my gut instinct. A tiger cannot change its stripes.

"How about we go inside and play a game?"

He shakes his head. "I want to wait out here."

"Sometimes things don't go the way you expect them to, remember?"

"Can you call Mommy?" he asks, refusing to accept the inevitable.

"She's not coming." There's no point in sugarcoating the truth.

"Maybe she's lost." He turns wide, sad eyes on me. "Call her."

"Okay," I concede, even though it won't make a difference. The call goes straight to voicemail.

"She didn't answer." It hurts to deliver the devastating news to him. "Let's go back inside." I stand, reaching for his hand.

"No!" he yells, racing down the stone driveway.

I run after him, easily catching up and lifting him into my arms.

"I'm so sorry, buddy."

"What's wrong with me?" He peers at me with sorrowful eyes. "If you tell her how helpful I am, she'll come."

His skinny arms encircle my neck as he cries his heart out. I carry him inside, shedding tears with him.

Cin

I finish my shower, grateful Art had a rainfall shower head installed in every bathroom in the house. My cell phone starts ringing as I step into my bedroom. It's probably Anneli. I'll give her a call once I'm done getting dressed. The ringing ends, then starts again in the next second. This better be important. I walk to the dresser and glance at the screen and see Art's name flash across it. He shouldn't be here for at least another hour and a half. I get up early enough to cook Mom and Sebastian breakfast before we walk him to school.

I press the speaker icon. "Hey."

"Mason is gone," Art says in a panic-stricken voice.

"What?" Those words cause immediate distress.

"I searched everywhere. He isn't here."

"Could he be hiding somewhere?"

There are many places Mason could conceal himself inside the mansion.

"He isn't here, goddamn it!" he bellows. "He took our bitch of a mother not showing pretty hard. I should've never let you convince me to give her a chance," he says accusingly.

"Art, I'm so—"

"Keep your fucking apology!" he shouts.

"I'll help you find him."

"I'm leaving for the police station now."

"Text me the address. I'll meet you there."

"No. Stay home."

"I'm not letting you do this alone, so please text me the damn address, Arthur!"

Art has me fucked up if he actually believes I'll be docile and follow his demand.

"That's the first time you've called me by my given name."

"I love that little boy as much as you do. I cannot sit and do nothing while he's missing. I will go to every police precinct in Orlando to find you. You don't think I feel like dog shit right now?" I cry. "He would be safe if you hadn't listened to me."

"Fuck, I shouldn't lash out at you." He takes a deep breath. "It's not your fault. I'm just so fucking scared."

"I'll be on the way in ten minutes."

"Okay."

I quickly dress, then race to my mom's room, but she's not there. I head downstairs.

"Mom!" I yell, barreling into the kitchen.

She yelps, turning from the coffee maker. "Cin, you nearly scared me to death."

"I need you to walk Sebastian to school alone."

"Did something happen?"

"There's no time to explain." I run towards the front door, grabbing my car keys along the way.

Art is out of his mind with worry. I've never heard him sound so afraid before. Whenever I try to do the right thing, I fuck it up. Maybe it's best if I keep my opinions to myself. Cursing my stupidity, I get in my car and speed off.

Damn, this light is taking forever to change!

I bite my fingernails, unable to control my nerves waiting for the traffic light to turn green. The drive seems to be taking forever. According to my GPS I should be at the police station in twenty-five minutes. I glance left, doing a double-take when I spot Mason sitting at the bus stop, crying, next to an elderly woman attempting to console him. I break down in tears, ecstatic he's safe. I make a U-turn and put the car in park before jumping out.

"Mason!"

He tears away from the woman and launches himself into my arms. "Cin!"

I'm squeezing him too tightly, but I can't help it. I plant kisses all over his face. "I'm so happy you're okay."

"Are you his mother?" the elderly woman asks. "He's so distraught, I couldn't get a word out of him."

"No, I know his brother. He's at the police station filing a missing person report."

"I saw the little guy sitting here upset and alone. I couldn't just walk by."

"Thank you so much for watching over him."

"You're welcome."

"Can I take you anywhere?"

"The offer is much appreciated, but I enjoy my daily walks."

"Okay. I'm going to take him home so he can get some rest."

"That's a good idea."

I put Mason in the back seat and buckle him in.

"Are you mad at me?"

"Of course not, silly."

"Is Art?"

"No, he's just really worried."

"But I left home by myself."

"That was a really dangerous thing to do. Something bad could've happened to you."

"I wanted to find Mommy."

"I know it makes you sad she isn't around, but it'll get better, I promise. You're a strong boy, and I'll be here to help."

"You'll never leave me, right? That's what Art said."

"You're so awesome. My life wouldn't be complete without you."

He laughs gleefully when I tickle him.

"There's the smile I love seeing." I close the door, then get into the driver's seat.

I send Art a text before pulling away, letting him know Mason is safe and sound.

ART

I take off at a dead run from the precinct after reading the text from Cin. It doesn't take me long to get home. I'm surprised I made it without being pulled over by the cops. I rush inside and up the stairs. I hear Cin's beautiful voice the closer I get to Mason's bedroom. I peer through the slightly open door. They lie on the bed together while she reads him a book. It's the same one I read at Cole's gravesite. The memory of that day flashes through my mind. I had fought going, but she pushed and wouldn't relent until I agreed to go. Since then, I've visited several times, bringing Mason along. I told him everything about Cole. I still haven't fully forgiven myself for his death, and most likely never will, but I've learned to live with it for Mason's sake. Cin brought me back from the brink. I would probably be six feet under if not for her. Those initial months together were the happiest of my life, which is why her betrayal cut so fucking deep. Eight years later and it still hasn't healed. That's a hell of a long time to hold a grudge. A normal person would've forgiven her and moved on, but I've never claimed to be normal. My name and that word don't belong in the same sentence. Abnormal? Now that word fits perfectly.

"Do you want me to read another book?" Cin asks Mason.

"No." He yawns.

"I bought this book for Cole's birthday, long ago."

"You knew my brother?"

"Yes, after he went to heaven."

"I wish he was still here."

"He is. You just can't see him."

I listen intently to their exchange. I want to believe there's a divine presence above, but so much fucked-up shit happens in the world, it's hard to.

"Are you hungry? I can whip you up some breakfast."

"I'm tired."

"Okay. I'll have something delicious ready for you by the time you wake up."

"I want pizza!"

"Pizza it is."

"Will you be my new mommy?" he asks hesitantly.

I hold my breath, waiting for her response.

"Absolutely, it'll be an honor. Thank you for choosing me."

"And Sebastian will be my real brother?"

"Yes."

"Yayyy!"

"All right." She gets out of the bed and pulls the comforter up to his chin. "Get some sleep."

"I love you, Cin."

"I love you too."

I move to the left to avoid being seen as she turns to leave the bedroom. She steps out into the hall, pulling the door shut behind her.

Her eyes widen, zeroing in on me. She backs up in alarm as I quickly stride towards her. "Art, please—"

I fist my hand in her hair and use the other to cover her mouth. "Shhh." I lick her ear. "I'm going to fuck the shit out of you."

I maneuver her backwards, pressing her into the wall. Sniffing her neck, I breathe in her sweet scent.

"I could just eat you up," I murmur.

Cin pushes her petite hands under my shirt, sliding them over my hard abs before unbuttoning my pants and tugging the zipper down. She pulls my dick free, stroking the thick length. Only her touch can bring the raging beast in my soul to heel. I take hold of her shirt and rip it down the middle, then lift her bra over her succulent breasts.

"Beautiful." I push the plentiful mounds together, sucking one nipple, then the other.

"I want your dick stretching my pussy," she moans.

"I'll do more than that. I'm going to crack you the fuck open and ruin you for other men."

"You've already ruined me for other men. Isn't it obvious? You're the only man I'll ever want."

I hoist her up, attacking her lips and invading her mouth with my tongue. She fervently returns the kiss. I carry her to my room and deposit her beside the bed. She's so fucking tiny compared to me. I tower over her, the top of her head barely reaching my shoulders.

"Get naked."

She watches me, seductively removing each article of clothing, teasing me, tormenting me. Cin's always been good at that. She lies back on the edge of the bed and spreads her legs. My eyes stray to the plump nub protruding from her swollen pussy lips. *Lord have motherfucking mercy.* I move between her thighs, grabbing my throbbing dick, and run the engorged head through her sopping slit. Fuck, it's so damn hot. She sucks on her index finger, twirling her tongue around the digit before gradually pulling it free and circling her clit. Alluring russet-colored eyes intently peer at me, waiting to witness the exact moment I snap.

"I want you to lose control," she whispers.

"Trust me, you don't want that."

"I do. Please, fuck me hard."

"On your knees," I demand.

She rolls over, then arches her back perfectly, displaying her nice round ass.

"Remember you asked for this." I ram forward, tearing through tight muscles.

"Ugh!" she cries out.

In pleasure or in pain, I'm not sure, but I don't give a fuck. I guess that truly does make me a monster. Cin pleaded for this, so she must face the consequences. My fingers dig into her hips, pulling her back to meet my violent thrusts. I ruthlessly plunge in and out of her exquisitely wet cunt, reveling in the sounds of her screams and the jiggle of her ass. She bleeds from where my nails press into her perfect silky skin. She reaches back, pressing her hand against my lower stomach, attempting to minimize the impact to her body.

"You begged the monster to come out and play, so fucking play," I growl, moving her hand.

My dick is completely covered in her white cream. *Juicy deliciousness, fuck.* I'm about to come. I can't tap out. She has to find release first. Slowing down, I pace myself, shaking with the effort not to pour my seed inside her. Damn, it's not working, I'm still about to explode. *Fuck!* Goddamn, her pussy is making me a weak little bitch.

"Come for me." I lightly pinch and pluck her fat clit, hoping she comes in the next few seconds because it's about to be a wrap for me.

I can't take it anymore. Each stroke moves me closer to fulfillment. I roar, unloading my semen in her paradise, and sweet merciful Jesus, her pussy squeezes my dick at the same time, signaling her climax.

"Oh God!" she shouts.

"Don't cry out for him. You cry out for me. I'm your God." I collapse on top of her, depleted.

I drag my ass up on the bed, tugging Cin to my side. She snuggles into me, laying her head on my chest and throwing her leg over mine.

"You want a shower?" I ask.

"I can barely move, so standing isn't an option," she replies. "I'm in need of a nap, but a quick one. I promised Mason pizza would be waiting for him when he wakes up."

"I'll order from Giuseppe's. They have the best pizza in Orlando."

"Okay. How did he get out of the house?"

"I never bothered activating the mansion's alarm system, but that'll change immediately. I'll have a serious talk with him later."

The gate has a motion sensor from the inside, so when he walked up it opened, or he squeezed through the bars. After I checked the kitchen and still hadn't found Mason, my heart dropped to the pit of my stomach. I was transported back to the day I found Cole's lifeless body in the pool and I feared the worst. Mason is a good swimmer, but he's far from advanced. It was a huge relief when he wasn't there either. Then I thought maybe my mother had something to do with his disappearance, but Logan confirmed she boarded a plane to Paris yesterday morning, so I ruled her out. Today the code will be changed and the alarm system activated every evening.

"You're right to blame me. This wouldn't have happened if it weren't for me." Tears spill from her eyes. "I swear if he'd gotten hurt…"

"You didn't force me to agree. I made the decision—"

"Your decision would've been different if I hadn't thrown in my two cents."

"You made a good point about giving her the chance to make amends. I did my part by doing right by my brother. My conscience is clear. Like you said, it's a hard lesson for Mason to learn, but it was necessary."

"I'm relieved he's safe."

"I heard you accept the responsibility of being Mason's mother. Did you mean it?"

"I wouldn't have said it if I didn't."

"Good."

Cin

It's been almost a week since Thanksgiving. Art and Mason came over for the holiday. Even though it was only us, I cooked a huge feast, so we'll be eating leftovers into the foreseeable future. Thank goodness there was no awkwardness at all. My mom has warmed up to Art and has fallen head over heels in love with Mason, calling him her second grandchild. She's been a bundle of energy ever since being offered a job as a sales associate at a department store. She cried when she found out. It's only a part-time seasonal position, but it means the world to her, and she may be asked to stay on permanently after Christmas. Anneli and I took her out to celebrate while Art looked after the boys. With Art's help, I surprised her with a new car. Now she can come and go as she pleases. Mason is doing better after the debacle his mother's reappearance caused. Two weeks have passed since that incident. I don't understand how a mother, or a father for that matter, can abandon their child. Unfortunately, Art and I are still at odds. I swear that man has mood swings like a woman on the rag, but our fucking is phenomenal. That's something I'll never complain about. Just when I think it can't get any more intense, he surprises me by turning up the heat another notch.

Clearing my mind, I try to focus on my current task. In my naïveté, I thought online shopping would be a great deal easier than actually going to a store. Boy was I wrong. Shopping and I are archenemies. Obviously the bitch has a vendetta against me, but she'll need to get in line behind Art. I'm about to bang my head against the coffee table, but instead I place the laptop on it and lean back against the soft cushions of the recliner. Mom is at work and Sebastian is in his bedroom. A sudden wave of queasiness assails me. This has become more and more frequent over the last couple of days. I close my eyes, willing the unpleasant feeling away. It's the turkey. Lord knows I've eaten like a glutton nonstop since Thursday.

I pop up in a panic as déjà vu hits me. While taking a shower earlier, I noticed my breasts were a little tender. These are some of the same symptoms I experienced during my first trimester with Sebastian. I haven't felt dizzy or vomited, but still, the similarities are too hard to ignore. *Stop it, Cin, you're being paranoid.* There's absolutely no way I'm pregnant. I specifically chose the Depo shot because I felt it's a more foolproof method of birth control, and I didn't want the added responsibility of taking a pill every day. A doctor would say the only way to prevent pregnancy is abstinence. Sure, I haven't had my period in two months, but my doctor assured me that it's normal for a woman's monthly cycle to stop even after only one injection. I'll just make an appointment to put my fears to rest. I refuse to think about it anymore and drive myself crazy.

My nerves wouldn't let me wait until morning to call my gynecologist's office, so I sent a message through the Contact Us option on the website last night, requesting the first available appointment. I didn't expect to receive a reply, but within an hour I was scheduled to come in the next day at nine. It didn't sit right with me not to discuss the possibility of being pregnant with Art, but there's no need to broach the subject until I'm one hundred percent certain. I sent Art a text instead of calling, letting him know I needed the day off because I'm not feeling well. Of course, he called until I answered, demanding I describe every symptom in detail. He was ready to cancel meetings and other scheduled engagements to see to my comfort. It took some time, but eventually I convinced him to continue with his day as planned.

I fidget on the examination table as Dr. Gates enters the room.

"Good morning," she greets, sitting on a stool.

I clear my throat. "Good morning."

"What brings you in today, Ms. Belo?"

"I think I may be pregnant."

"Did you take a pregnancy test?"

"Well, no. I prefer a blood test, just to be one hundred percent positive."

"Sure, but a urine test can be done too if you'd like. The choice is yours."

"I'd rather not panic until absolutely necessary." I laugh nervously.

"Trust me, I understand your trepidation. Just having a blood test done is fine," she assures me. "What are your symptoms?"

"Nausea and my breasts are sensitive."

"When did this start?"

"About a week ago."

"Have you been feeling fatigued?"

"Not really."

"What about morning sickness?"

"Nope. Do you think I'm being overdramatic?"

"No, making an appointment was a smart move on your part so we can get to the bottom of the sudden changes you're experiencing."

"I read that only three in one thousand women will get pregnant while on the birth control shot."

"That's true. The failure rate is less than one percent."

"Aren't I lucky," I say sarcastically.

"You have options—"

"I'm keeping my baby, if there is one."

"Good. I should have the results in two to three business days."

"Tomorrow is Friday, so I won't know until Wednesday at the latest? That's a long wait." I'm going to go bonkers.

"I'll put a rush on the order so it's back by tomorrow, and I'll personally give you a call once the results are in."

I'm so happy Art recommended Dr. Gates. She's professional, super nice, and attentive.

"Thank you so much."

"You're welcome."

"How did you and Art meet?" I ask.

Her demeanor changes, and she looks uneasy. "Through mutual acquaintances."

That's weird. Her lack of a detailed response and her tone brooked no further conversation on the topic. Did my question upset her? If so, I wonder why? They couldn't have dated. She's almost old enough to be his grandmother, so why the abrupt change over a simple inquiry?

"Again, thanks for all your help today. I truly appreciate it."

She nods her head, leaving the room. Her reaction is strange as hell. What is going on? I'll revisit this later. I have bigger fish to fry in my life, like the possible bun baking in my oven.

As I settle into my car, a new thought flashes through my mind. What if Art doesn't want our baby? My heart would rip in two. Having one baby daddy who isn't interested in his child is a nightmare, but two would be a damn tragedy. How will Mom and Anneli take the news? I can't stress myself out. Not in my condition.

Condition?

God, I'm acting like the pregnancy is confirmed. Tomorrow can't get here soon enough. I'd rather stay home and wait for the phone call, but Art will become suspicious if I miss work two days in a row. It'll be difficult acting like nothing is wrong around him. I'm going to be on pins and needles until Dr. Gates calls.

Cin

"You're quiet today." Art brings his car to a stop in front of the mansion.

We were almost at our destination when Art realized he forgot the USB needed for this morning's meeting.

"I'm not accustomed to talking unless there's something to talk about."

He eyes me suspiciously. "How are you feeling?"

"Great. It was just a twenty-four-hour bug, nothing serious."

"You sure?"

"Yeah. I'm right as rain."

His unwavering gaze nearly has me blurting out the real reason I missed work yesterday.

"Give me a few minutes," he says, leaving the car.

"Okay." I check my cell phone, hoping to see a missed call from Dr. Gates, though it's still early.

After a few minutes turns into several, I go inside to search for Art. Maybe he needs help finding the USB. I follow the sound of his muffled voice to his study. His words become clearer the closer I get to the door, which has been left slightly ajar.

"Are you sure she's pregnant?"

I can't believe what I'm hearing. Did he conspire to purposely get me pregnant? Dr. Gates's sudden change in demeanor makes perfect sense now. Fucking bastard!

"Good. I'll have the money transferred to your account."

Am I in the fucking twilight zone? I storm through the door and grab the vase off a nearby table. Art turns around just as I launch it straight towards his fucking head. He throws up his arm, blocking the impact. My preferred target was his beautiful masculine face, but a sense of gratification flows through me as blood pours from the cut on his forearm.

"I'll call you back." He puts the cell phone in his pocket. "That's a twenty-thousand-dollar vase."

"Fuck the vase!" I yell. "This is the second time you've done something to my body without my permission!"

He points at a blood stain on his shirt. "This is one of my favorite shirts."

"You're an egomaniac on a power trip."

He shrugs his shoulders, cool as a goddamn cucumber. "Thanks for the compliment."

I charge at him in a blind rage. He laughs, deflecting each blow as if I were nothing more than a bothersome fly.

"Your behavior isn't good for the baby." He grabs my wrists, preventing me from scratching out his eyeballs. "The health of our unborn child should be your number one concern."

I go full apeshit on his ass, kicking and swinging, trying my best to hurt him. The fucker must have been a gladiator in his past life. He picks me up, holding me like a sack of potatoes.

I struggle to break away. "What was in the shot that bitch gave me?"

"It was harmless," he says, dumping me onto the sofa.

I scramble to the other end. "Tell me!"

"A saline solution," he answers, undoing his slacks.

"What the hell are you doing?"

"All this fighting made me horny as fuck."

"You're crazy if you think I'm going to have sex with you!"

"You should realize by now that whatever I want is mine, by any means necessary."

"A victory gained by force is hollow."

"I beg to differ. A victory, especially one gained by force, is the sweetest aphrodisiac." Art latches onto my ankles and drags me across the sofa. I sit up, slapping him across the face. He pushes me back, pinning my wrists above my head with one hand.

"Keep fighting. It makes my dick harder." He pries my thighs apart, then settles between them, pressing me into the cushions with his heavy weight.

"I hope you burn in hell," I grind out. "Does having power over me make you feel like a big strong man?"

"It's almost better than coming deep in your pussy," he says, licking me from my chin to my forehead.

"You're a weak, pathetic excuse of a human being."

"You can pretend you're not enjoying every single minute, but—" His hand slips under my dress and pushes into my panties, easily penetrating my center.

I bite my tongue to silence my moan. He slowly withdraws, lifting two glistening fingers to my face, showing me what I already know. *I'm wet as shit.*

"This doesn't lie." He brings his fingers to his nose and inhales deeply before lapping them clean. "So fucking tasty."

"Can I taste?"

Art opens his mouth, presenting his tongue, and I eagerly suck on it as he enters my body. He fucks me slow, tenderly—not hard, which is his usual method, but the effect on me is just as profound. This is different. A claiming. He's making love to me for the first time, and I bask in it. It's too overpowering—every thrust, every sensual kiss—God help me. Is it possible to die from extreme pleasure?

"You're crying." He licks my tears.

"Let me go."

"No."

"Please, I need to touch you."

He releases my wrists, allowing me free rein. I pay homage to the sleek muscles of his arms and back.

"Look at me."

The intensity reflecting in his sparkling green eyes is overwhelming.

"You feel it too," I whisper.

"I've always felt it."

I fall over the edge and he follows behind me. We hold each other, sated and breathless.

"It's true what they say."

"About what?"

"Pussy is riper during pregnancy."

"How much did you pay her?"

"She's set for the rest of her life."

"Why did you do it?"

"I want you to have my baby."

"That's not a decision you make on your own, Art!"

"It's done. Get over it."

"This isn't about you wanting me to be the mother of your child. You want complete control over me."

"What's wrong with that?"

"Having another baby without a ring on my finger is not an ideal situation for me."

He pulls out of me and walks over to his desk. I remain on my back, legs spread wide with his cum trickling to the crack of my ass. He rummages through the drawer, then returns holding something.

"What is that?" I ask, moving to a sitting position.

He grabs my hand and slips the largest diamond I've ever seen onto my finger.

"Is this your way of asking me to marry you?"

"I'm not asking."

"You're making a hell of an assumption."

"You don't have a choice."

"I won't be forced into a marriage."

"You're going to do exactly what I want." His self-assurance grates on my nerves. "Resistance is futile. In a few months, your name will be Cinnamon King."

"What you and Dr. Gates did is highly illegal…" I pause for dramatic effect. "Maybe I'll contact the DA. You both could go to prison for a very long time."

"Be my guest. You don't have any proof."

"Your phone records and bank statements can be subpoenaed."

"Do you think I'm stupid enough to use a cell phone and bank account that can be traced back to me?" He laughs. "Come on. Give me some credit."

"Swiss bank account? How many illegal dealings are you involved in?"

"The Falcon name wouldn't be what it is today if only squeaky-clean tactics were used." He smirks. "You have five minutes to clean yourself up. Thanks to you, we're going to be late for the meeting."

"Me? You really are a piece of work."

"You're not allowed in my study again." He nods towards the blood and semen stains on the cream-colored sofa. "You ruined my sofa and broke my vase."

"And you conspired with my doctor to get me pregnant. So yeah, my grievance is more severe than yours."

"I'm willing to do whatever it takes to keep you." The ferocity of his tone leaves me breathless. "You belong to me and always will. God help anyone who tries to take you from me."

"I'm not a possession."

He stoops until we're at eye level. "Property of Arthur King is stamped on your ass."

"That doesn't make me yours."

"But it does." He places his large palm on my flat belly. "I would die for this baby, and it isn't even born yet. Don't fight this. You won't win. Start making preparations for a wedding." He walks out of the study.

Silence fills the car as Art drives me home later that evening.

"What about our living situation?" I ask.

"You and Sebastian are moving in with me. We'll transfer him to the school Mason attends next year."

"What about my mom?"

"Your mother can stay in the house. It's hers, or she can come too."

This is all happening so fast, my head is spinning.

"My lawyer will draw up paperwork for me to legally adopt Sebastian and for you to adopt Mason. We're going to be a family."

"What?"

"I already consider him my son, and Mason wants you to be his mother."

"Trevor never relinquished his parental rights."

"I'll take care of it."

"What are you planning to do?"

"It doesn't concern you."

"How do you expect us to have a successful marriage if you shut me out? You can't make decisions on your own."

"I'm going to pay him a visit."

"I want to go too."

"No."

"I'm coming."

"No, the fuck you're not!" he shouts. "I don't want you near him. I'll take care of all the details."

"That's not how a marriage works."

"It's how this one will."

"The hell it is."

"He hates you and Sebastian. You have no reason to see him again."

"It's been eight years. There's a chance he'll be more accepting of Sebastian."

"Has he even reached out to you once?"

"No," I admit.

"If he had a change of heart, he would have. You and Sebastian are my responsibility now. I will be good to him and our baby."

"What about me? Will you be good to me too?"

"I will once you admit the truth and spend the rest of your life making it up to me."

"I'll never admit to something I didn't do."

"Then you have your answer."

"It's not healthy to hold a grudge for this long."

"Neither is eating a juicy sirloin saturated in butter, but I'm still going to fucking eat it."

This man is so goddamn infuriating, but I love him with my stupid ass, even after everything he's done. I'm an idiot.

Cin

Peering around the table, I anxiously watch my mom and Anneli as they enjoy brunch. I suggested we go out under the guise of having girl time, but in reality, I felt the need to disclose the news of my pregnancy in public so they'd be forced to keep their voices low. The engagement ring is hidden in my bedroom away from their prying eyes.

"Are you going to eat or spend the entire time looking at your mother and me?"

"Just spit it out," Mom says.

"I'm pregnant," I blurt.

Neither one responds to the announcement.

"Say something, please."

"How long have you known?" Mom asks.

"Just two days."

"Art is the father." The disappointment in Anneli's voice is clear.

Though it's not a question, I answer anyway. "He is."

"This is unbelievable." Anneli slams her fork down. "I thought you were on birth control."

"It didn't work." *Because Art paid the doctor to sabotage the shot.*

"What's going to happen now?" Mom asks.

"We're getting married."

"Don't be stupid." Anneli throws her arms up in frustration. "I kept my mouth shut about the six-month agreement, but enough is enough!"

"Cin, what is Anneli talking about?"

The clawing cat is finally out of the bag. "We'll discuss it later, Mom."

"I refuse to witness your self-destruction. Art is like a parasite. He latched onto you and is slowly filling your body with poison."

"You promised to be here for me."

"I was hoping you'd come to your senses!"

"I'm going to have his baby."

"That doesn't mean you have to marry him!" Anneli yells.

"I love him."

"Love is truly blind." Anneli storms out of the restaurant.

"Well, what do you have to say about it?"

She leans over, wiping away a stray tear rolling down my cheek. "I want you to be happy, and Art can't give you that, not truly. How can you have a future with him when he's living in the past?"

"We'll make it work."

"For how long? I'm not going to try to change your mind. I may not agree with your decision, but I'll support you, regardless."

I wrap my arms around her in a tight hug. "Thanks, Mom."

"Give Anneli a few days. She'll come around."

I hate that she's disappointed in me. Once she calms down, she'll be ecstatic about having another godchild.

ART

"What's taking her so fucking long?" I pace the small room impatiently.

"Can you have a seat, please?"

"No."

"The poor ultrasound tech is going to take one look at you and run screaming from the room."

"It's been twenty-five minutes already," I growl.

"More like fifteen."

I've known this day was coming for a week, but I'm still not prepared. We're going to get the first glimpse of our baby today. I'm scared shitless. Fuck, I'm going to be a father. Babies are so goddamn tiny. I avoided holding Mason as an infant, scared he would wiggle right out of my arms. Cin refused to make an appointment with the obstetrician I chose, swearing never to go to anyone I recommended for anything ever again. Eventually, we compromised. Though this doctor isn't the best in the area, she's among the top three. The boys were thrilled when we told them the news. Of course, they want a little brother. I don't care what the sex of our new addition to the family is. I just want a healthy baby. I haven't told the old man or Josh about my pending fatherhood, and I don't plan to for now. The last thing I need is for them to be in my business, giving unwanted advice. The door opens and a middle-aged Asian woman steps inside.

"Mr. King and Ms. Belo, please accept my apologies for the delay."

"Your apology is not—"

"Truly it's no problem at all," Cin says, cutting off my tirade.

I sit in the chair next to the examination table.

"My name is Ling Hong, but you're welcome to call me Ling."

She asks Cin a plethora of questions, leaving my mind a little warped. I'm completely out of my element.

"A transvaginal ultrasound will need to be performed."

"What's that?" I ask. "All of this is new to me, so I'd appreciate it if you explained every step."

"Sure. It's a wand inserted into the vaginal canal. Per the first day of Ms. Belo's last period, I'm guessing she's maybe six weeks pregnant. At this stage the fetus is only the size of a sweet pea, so this is the best way to have a clear visual inside the uterus and determine overall development."

I nod, acknowledging my understanding.

"Undress from the waist down and cover yourself with this." She hands Cin a disposal drape. "I'll give you some privacy," she says, leaving the room.

I slap Cin on the ass when she bends over to remove her panties.

"Will you stop it?" She giggles, swatting at me.

"Well, you shouldn't have put it in my face."

"Keep it up and I'll have you thrown out," she threatens, lying back on the examination table and covering herself.

"All set?" Ling calls through the door.

"Yes," Cin answers.

She comes back into the room.

"All right, let's take a peek at your bundle of joy." Ling covers the wand with a condom and gel. "Are you ready?"

"Ready as I'll ever be."

"Count to three, then take a deep breath. You're going to feel a little pressure."

"One, two, three."

"See? That wasn't too hard."

A rapid thumping sound echoes throughout the room.

"That's our baby's heartbeat." I kiss Cin's belly.

"And a strong one it is," Ling says.

I know I'm sporting the same silly grin as Cin.

Ling points at the screen. "Here is the chorionic and yolk sac. And this bean shape is the fetal pole."

"It's amazing," I say in awe.

"The next ultrasound will be in three months. It'll be transabdominal. Also, if you both would like, I can disclose the sex of your baby at that time. The head, torso, and limbs will be visible as well."

"That's an eternity." I'll be like a kid waiting for Christmas morning.

"Is this your first child?"

"Biologically speaking. It shows, huh?"

"Yes." She laughs.

"I can't wait to meet you," Cin says, rubbing her stomach.

We ask Ling a few more questions before being given a due date and ultrasound images. I have no second thoughts or remorse for engaging in sneaky underhanded tactics to get what I wanted. I'd do it again in the blink of an eye. Cin's misgivings about how she became pregnant evaporated when she heard our baby's heartbeat. She's already in love and so am I.

Twenty-nine

Cin

Spending the last several hours at the mall has left me fatigued and hungry. Since shopping online didn't work out for me, a trip to this nightmare was in order. The worst part was undertaking the task alone. Art left for Las Vegas two days ago to help Josh with a business deal. I couldn't chance the boys catching a glimpse of their Christmas presents, so Mom stayed home to watch them. And Anneli—we've spoken since the bombshell was delivered, but she's having a difficult time processing my pregnancy and impending wedding. I understand she needs space, so I didn't ask her to join me. She relented and called after I sent her a picture of the sonogram. Anneli wants all of this for me, just not with Art. She's adamant in her belief he'll hurt me. I can't have my best friend and husband at odds.

Hopefully they'll find common ground soon. My mom ranted and raved as I described the details of my sordid arrangement with Art. It wasn't an easy conversation to have. I make my way swiftly down the street towards a Portuguese restaurant. I'm too tired to go home and cook, so this is the next best thing.

"Cin." I look back to see Adrian approaching.

Panic sets in before I remember Art isn't even in the state, meaning there's no chance he could appear and cause a scene like at the school.

"I thought that was you," he says.

"Hey. It's been a long time."

"You look good."

"Thank you. You're not looking too bad yourself."

"Where you headed?"

"I need food, ASAP."

"Me too. Mind if I join you?"

"That's probably not a good idea."

"I want to apologize for the way I acted the last time we saw each other."

"Oh, it's fine. Really."

"It isn't. I shouldn't have forced myself on you. I kind of lost it for a second, but that's still no excuse for my behavior."

"All is forgiven. I'm sorry for the way I ended things between us."

"Make it up to me by allowing me to treat you to lunch," he pushes, determined not to let me off the hook. "We can go wherever you want."

"I don't know."

"We're just two old friends catching up, nothing more."

"Okay."

There's nothing wrong with us sharing a meal. It's harmless.

"Where are we going?"

"A Portuguese spot, it's around the next corner."

"Sounds good."

We walk down the street together, making idle conversation.

"I hear congratulations are in order."

"Anneli told you I'm pregnant?" I can't believe she did that.

"No. You're going to have a baby? Wow," he says, unsuccessfully hiding his dismay.

"What were you referring to then?"

"I noticed the engagement ring on your finger."

"Oh." I'm not used to wearing the blasted thing. "I always forget it's there."

"A rock that size is hard to miss."

"It is pretty huge."

"When is the big day?"

"We haven't chosen one yet."

"So, I've truly lost you."

"Adrian—"

"I was thinking out loud."

"I didn't mean to hurt you."

"The heart wants what it wants, right?" He softly brushes the side of my face.

I step back. "Don't."

"You can't blame me for needing to touch you one last time."

"I'd better go."

"Stay." He waves his hand towards the entrance to the restaurant. "We're here."

"What are you expecting?" It wouldn't be fair to lead him on.

"Only your company for a meal. You can at least give me that."

"Okay." Guilt makes me give in.

ART

Once the meeting in Las Vegas concluded, I headed to San Francisco. It turns out Trevor remained in California after graduating college. He readily accepted my invitation to meet at the Falcon located downtown, which doesn't surprise me in the least. He has an angle, but I've played this game before. I invented it. There's no doubt in my mind I'll come out the victor. I know everything about him, down to his credit score. The motherfucker was supposed to be here a half hour ago. I detest tardiness.

The office phone rings. "Yes."

"Mr. Trevor Brooks is here to see you," the front desk clerk says.

"Thank you. Send him in please."

"Yes, sir."

He struts in, smug and disinterested. The fucker is putting on a show already.

"Trevor."

His appearance hasn't changed much, though his facial features are a bit worn.

"Arthur." He drops into the chair and crosses his ankles on the desk—displaying complete disrespect. Dirt and debris from his shoes fall to the gleaming oak surface.

"To what do I owe the pleasure?"

Opening the drawer, I retrieve a folder containing the adoption documents and slide it in front of him.

"What do we have here?" He peruses the contents. "So, you want to be the little bastard's father?"

"Call him that again and I'll break every bone in your fucking body."

He laughs. "Boy, she has her hooks in you."

"Sign the document."

"Maybe I don't want to." He throws the folder on the desk. "Maybe it's about time I step up and play daddy."

"You'll give me what I want."

"What makes you so sure?"

"You're on the brink of filing for bankruptcy."

His indifferent attitude disappears promptly.

"No flippant comeback."

Checkmate.

"Your small IT company is drowning in debt." I pull my checkbook from my breast pocket and toss it on the desk. "Money is your motivation for agreeing to meet me today."

He licks his lips. "I want five million and he's yours."

"Half a million."

"Three million."

"This isn't a negotiation. You take the offer or you leave here with nothing."

"No deal."

"Then this conversation is over." I turn my attention to my laptop. "You can go."

"Okay," he relents, greed getting the best of him.

He leans over and provides his signature for the required sections while I fill out the check. "There, all done." He throws the pen down. "Are you and Cin getting married?"

"We are. She's pregnant."

He eagerly grabs the check I hold out to him. "I got the better end of the deal. I'm now legally rid of him, and I have the funds to save my company."

"I pity you if you believe that."

"The probability of you not being the father of that baby is great. It's you who needs pitying," he says, leaving the office.

I truly dislike the asshole, but I can't blame him for his bitterness. Not when it's been my constant companion for all these years. That girl has wrecked us both. She cast a spell, and it remains strong to this very day. Still, he's a weak man for abandoning his son because of his hate for her. I could never do that. I check my cell phone when I receive a notification.

Logan: You have an important email.

Cin

After enduring Sebastian and Mason's shenanigans all day, I'm exhausted. The boys are a handful separately, but together they make an unstoppable force. Their energy is contagious, but I can only handle so much of it. Mom took over the reins, allowing me to shower and head to bed early. My cell phone chimes as I snuggle under the comforter.

Art: Be at the penthouse in an hour.

Me: Why?

Ten minutes later, still no reply, so I shoot off another text.

Me: ???

The message remains unanswered. Apprehension slithers through my veins, leaving me cold. It doesn't bode well that he wants to meet there. Something must've happened while he was away. Next, I try calling, but each call is sent straight to voicemail. I get out of bed, steeling myself for my visit to the devil's lair.

Identical to my first visit, the elevator doors slide open revealing a dark interior. Will he pounce on me the moment I exit my coveted sanctuary?

"Art?" I lean out of the elevator, surveying the area. "Where are you?"

I tentatively step one foot out, then the other. Nothing. But experience has taught me never to let my guard down when it comes to Art.

I move forward. "This isn't funny."

The unknown has my imagination running wild. I wish he would appear and put me out of my damn misery already.

"Stop fucking around, Art!" I click the light switch, but it doesn't work. Inspecting further, I notice the light bulb is missing. Goose bumps prickle my cool skin. I go into the kitchen, looking for anything I can use for protection. I settle on the coffee pot before walking up the stairs, ready to strike if need be. Prepared for a life-and-death battle, I enter the bedroom, but the crazy man is nowhere in sight. At least the bright moon shining in through the window provides some visibility. Something on the bed catches my eye.

Oh my God.

Beside a thick rope are photos of Adrian and me on the day we had lunch together. We mirror a happy couple enjoying a nice day. This is bad.

"When the cat is away, the mice will play." His low menacing voice sends chills to my core.

I swing around, facing an angry, naked Art. Though I'm scared shitless, I can appreciate his magnificence. "You had me followed."

"I knew you couldn't be trusted."

"It's not what it seems," I say, pointing at the photos.

"You're caught red-handed, but yet you continue to lie!" he shouts.

"You need to listen to me," I say pleadingly. "We ran into each other on the street, and he asked me to join him for lunch. That's all."

He moves past me and plucks a photo from the bed. He holds up the one with Adrian caressing my face. "A picture is worth a thousand words."

"In this case, it doesn't tell the whole truth."

"Is the baby mine?"

"What?"

"You heard me."

"How can you ask me that?"

He strikes, quick as a snake, and circles his large hand around my throat in a painful hold. He effortlessly takes the coffee pot from my grasp and places it on the floor. "Once a whore, always a fucking whore," he sneers, slamming me onto the bed.

I cough, struggling to pull oxygen into my burning lungs.

"A paternity test will be taken immediately after birth. I swear I'll fucking kill you if I'm not the father."

"This is your baby!" I croak.

He grabs my wrists, using the rope to bind them tightly to the bedpost.

"You can't spank me." The coarse material digs into my flesh. "You could harm the baby."

"Physical pain is too good for you." He kisses my forehead. "You deserve mental anguish."

"You'll regret this later."

"I fell for you hard. Fuck, eight damn years later and I'm still falling."

A scantily dressed woman walks into the room. "Are you ready for me?" she asks seductively.

"Perfect timing."

"Who is she?" I ask, alarmed.

"Come." Art beckons her. "Get on the bed."

"Your wish is my command, Daddy."

"Get on your hands and knees, facing her."

"I'll hate you forever if you do this," I threaten.

He takes a condom from the nightstand and tears it open with his teeth before sheathing himself.

"Watch her while I fuck you," he instructs the woman, moving behind her.

"No!" I wail as tears flood my eyes.

He begins fucking her and the anguish he spoke of fills my soul, breaking me. I squeeze my eyes shut, but it doesn't lessen the agony. Every grunt and moan is equivalent to a gunshot to the chest.

"Open your damn eyes!"

"No," I sob.

Finally, the noises cease and the weight on the bed shifts, indicating the conclusion of my nightmare. Or is it the beginning?

"Call me anytime, sugar," the woman purrs.

"Leave, now," Art sneers, dismissing her.

"Asshole," she says, stomping from the room.

I hear movement, then the shower running. I'm not sure how much time goes by before the water is shut off.

"Now you know how it feels for the person you love to give a piece of themselves to someone else."

I work up the nerve to open my eyes, finding Art standing in front of me. He's no longer naked.

"At least you washed the skank's stench off," I say in disgust.

"You brought this on yourself." He unties me. "Don't expect remorse from me."

I reach down, take hold of the coffee pot, and smash it over his head. "Burn in hell!" I yell, fleeing the room.

"Cin!" he bellows.

Shit. He should've been knocked out cold. I make it into the elevator and press the button to close the doors. "Come on!"

I scream as Art comes barreling towards me, a murderous expression on his blood-covered face. I shrink back against the wall but thank goodness I'm ensconced in safety before he reaches me. Slumping to the floor, I give way to grief, crying uncontrollably. When the doors open, I make a mad dash for my car.

"Get back here!" Art roars, bursting from the stairwell.

Fuck, he's right on my heels. I jump inside my car and speed out of the garage. In my state, I don't notice the red light until it's too late. Tires screech, horns blare, metal crunches, and then blackness.

Cin

A beeping sound penetrates my foggy brain. *Where am I?* I'm stiff and sore all over. As I become more lucid, a disinfectant scent assails my nostrils. It smells like a hospital. Memories begin to filter through my muddled mind. I was in a car accident. I move my arm, causing a pained sound to escape my dry lips. The right side of my torso hurts like hell.

"I think she's waking," Anneli says.

My eyes flutter open. It takes a second for my blurry vision to clear.

"Thank God you're okay." She leans over my prone form, wiping tears from her face.

"Oh, sweetheart, we were so worried." Mom appears at my other side.

My heart skips a beat when my gaze lands on Art sitting in a chair at the foot of the bed. Cuts cover the left side of his face. *Good.*

"Get out!" I yell.

"I'm not going anywhere." He stands, crossing his arms.

"I want him gone, now!" I cry.

"Art, you should go," Mom says. "This isn't good for her."

"I don't mean any disrespect, but Cin is my fiancée, and she's carrying my child. I have a right to be here."

"My baby." I clutch my stomach.

"Is fine and healthy," Anneli assures me.

I take off the engagement ring and throw it at him. "Unfortunately, you are the father of my baby, but I'm no longer your fiancée. I'll never forgive you."

"We'll see about that." He retrieves the ring and puts it in his pocket. "Karma should've bitten you in the ass a long time ago."

I scream at the top of my lungs, trying to get out of the bed, but Mom and Anneli hold me down.

"Art, please just leave," Anneli begs.

A nurse comes into the room, alerted by the commotion.

"What's going on?" she asks.

"My daughter wants him to go," Mom says, nodding towards Art.

"Sir, security will be notified if you refuse to leave on your own."

"Cin, I'll give you space for now, but don't think for a minute this is over," he states, exiting the room.

"Go to hell!" I struggle to draw in breath.

"What's wrong with her?" Anneli asks.

"She needs rest," the nurse answers.

"Is she going to be okay?" Mom asks in alarm.

"Yes, I'll be back with a mild sedative to calm her down."

My strength begins to wane, then darkness overtakes me again.

ART

I royally fucked up. Being only seconds behind her, I saw the car accident happen. Time stood still. There was nothing I could do but watch in horror as her vehicle was struck before fishtailing. I raced towards the mangled metal, petrified of what I would find inside. She was unconscious—the only visible sign of injury a knot forming at her right temple. Relief flooded me when I felt a strong, steady pulse. I didn't pull her from the wreckage, afraid of making any internal injuries worse, so I dialed 911 and waited for paramedics to arrive. Once she was stabilized and packed into the ambulance, I called her mom. Heather was available to watch Sebastian and Mason so Missy could meet me at the hospital.

Instead of going home after being dismissed from the hospital, I drive to Adrian's house to lie in wait for him. I could be making a bad situation a lot fucking worse, but I need answers and I can't trust her to be honest. History is repeating itself. Except this time, I'm not the other man. Cin is good at making me spiral out of control. I twirl the engagement ring in my fingers. It'll be returned to its rightful owner soon enough. The bastard's finally home. I'm across the street and on him the moment he exits his vehicle, delivering a brutal gut punch. He doubles over, wheezing, and being the sadistic prick that I am, I hit him a second time for good measure.

"You fucking my girl?" I growl.

"What if I am?" He smirks.

I deck him in the mouth for that comeback. "I can make you disappear."

"I'm not afraid of you."

I pull a knife from my pocket and tap it between his legs. "And here I thought you were smart."

"Take it easy." His tune changes instantly.

"Do you want to have children one day?" He tenses as I press the blade into his crotch harder.

"Crazy asshole."

"You know this, and yet you continue to fuck with me." I apply more pressure. "I'm waiting on a goddamn answer."

"We've never fucked."

"Never?"

"No."

"What kind of fool do you take me for?" I put the knife against his throat, pressing until blood trickles down his neck.

He winces. "It's the truth."

"If I find out—"

"She wanted to take it slow."

Either she's been telling the truth this whole time or they're both pros at deception.

"Ever go near her again and I'll give you a vasectomy."

"You're a sick son of a bitch."

"I am *the* son of a bitch, so I can't be upset at that comment. As for being sick, I own that too." I slide the knife in my pocket. "Remember what I said. Stay far away from my girl," I say, delivering one more gut punch for the hell of it.

I get in my car and contemplate my next move. Going back to the hospital is out of the question. Surely, Cin will scream her head off and have security throw my ass out on the curb. I'll allot her twenty-four hours to calm down, but that's it. She needs to get the hell over it and fast. I fucked another woman, so what? Cin isn't innocent in all this. She's no stranger to infidelity—throwing stones in glass houses and all that shit. I gave her specific instructions to avoid him at all costs. She had no business having lunch with the fucker. The lesson was hard, but she had to be taught. She'll either obey me now or hate me more. I don't care which as long as she's mine.

Cin

I come to, stretching my sore body. Anneli is snuggled against my side, fast asleep. I shake her shoulder until she wakes up.

"Welcome back to the land of the living." She yawns, sitting up. "How are you feeling?"

"Like I've been drugged," I say groggily.

"It had to be done to get your breathing and heart rate under control."

"Where's Sebastian?"

"At home with your mom."

"Mason?"

"Art has him."

"Were they at the hospital?"

"No, Heather looked after them."

"Do they know about the car accident?"

"Yes. They're upset they couldn't see you."

I'll call them, but first I need water for my parched throat. "I need water."

"Okay. I'll get you a bottle from the vending machine."

She returns, handing me the cold drink. "It's clear something happened between you and Art. How did he get those cuts on his face?"

"He did something awful." Fat tears roll down my face.

"What did he do?"

"I'm not ready to talk about it."

"Okay. Is it really over?"

"I think it is."

"You'll need to get a restraining order."

"What?"

"You know he's not going to leave you alone."

"No, I will not abandon Mason no matter what Art and I are going through. He has been hurt enough, and I made a promise to always be there for him. And I'm having Art's baby. I would never keep him from his child. Sebastian adores him and they have a strong bond. I would never deny them that. He may not be good to me, but he's good to him."

"He's obsessed with you and that makes him dangerous. Do you honestly think he's going to let you live your life freely and date other men?"

"I'll figure it out."

"You're lucky to be alive."

"He didn't cause the car accident."

"But he's the reason it happened. I know he is. You walked away with scrapes, bruises, and a concussion, but it could've been so much worse."

"Anneli, I'll handle this," I say sternly, effectively ending the conversation. "I need to call the boys."

Art will come at me with every weapon in his arsenal. The question is—will I be able to resist him?

ART

Cin has eluded me since the day of the car accident. I have yet to catch her alone. She's either with her mother or Anneli, and those two won't let me near her. They're like pit bulls protecting their pup. During each confrontation, Cin remains silent, not speaking one word to me. They handle all phone conversations and text messages. She has completely cut me off. Mason asked why Sebastian comes over but not Cin. I told him we need some time apart. That explanation will have to suffice. She even changed the house locks on me. Anneli alluded to a restraining order being filed against me if I continue coming by unannounced. Having that on my record could cause problems for me. To avoid involving the courts, I grudgingly admit temporary defeat while contemplating my next course of action.

I still make sure she's straight—all her bills paid. She has a new car too. Being deprived of her smell, her touch, her pussy… is motherfucking torture. I fucking miss her. Jerking off every damn day to the memory of her body is nowhere near enough to sate my sexual appetite. My dick is raw and chafed from the abuse it has endured. I swear to God the moment I get Cin alone, I'm going to fuck her so savagely, her screams will be heard across the East Coast. Only two-and-a-half weeks and I'm already a ticking time bomb. She's lost her goddamn mind if she believes I'll allow her to walk away from me. It'll be a cold day in hell.

Now here it is, Christmas Eve, and I'm alone. Mason is with Cin. Though it's half past noon, I haven't left my bed. I'll be spending the holiday alone. Tomorrow, they're traveling to North Carolina to visit family and friends and won't return until after the New Year. I was supposed to be going with them until this fucking mess.

The security alarm comes blaring to life. I react instantly, jumping from the bed and retrieving my Glock from the safe in my closet. Stark naked, I move down the stairs quietly, cocking the weapon and placing my finger on the trigger—ready to empty the clip into the person stupid enough to break into my residence. Never invade a man's home. That's a cardinal rule for survival in these streets. I turn the corner, pressing the barrel of the gun to Josh's forehead. He holds his hands up in surrender.

"This is the welcome I get for coming to spend Christmas with you?"

"You must have a death wish. I could've killed you." I tilt my head to the side. "I still might. You broke into my home uninvited, which is enough probable cause to empty the clip into you."

"Don't joke about something like that and stop pointing the damn thing at my head!"

"Who says I'm joking?" I raise an eyebrow.

"Mr. King, is police assistance needed?" a voice comes from the security pad.

Releasing the trigger, I click on the safety before walking over to press a button on the square-shaped device. "False alarm."

"Please provide the security passcode."

I rattle off the numbers.

"You're all set, Mr. King. Is there anything else I can do for you?"

"No."

"Have a great day, sir."

"You too," I say and release the button.

"She has a sex phone operator's voice." Josh grins. "I need her number."

"The gate code was changed." I face him. "How did you get in?"

"I climbed over it and let me tell you, I almost broke my neck."

"It looks like Santa Claus didn't read my letter this year."

"Very funny."

"And just how did you get inside here?"

"I broke a window," he answers sheepishly.

"I do have a doorbell," I deadpan.

"You wouldn't have opened the door for me," he scoffs.

"I'm not in the mood for company." I stroll towards the kitchen, intent on satisfying my hunger. I haven't eaten all day.

"Aren't you going to put some clothes on?"

"Close your eyes if you don't want to see."

"Our grandfather is worried about you and so am I. You've gone completely MIA."

"That's because I want to be left the fuck alone."

"Well, had you at least returned one call or text, I wouldn't have come."

"As you can see, I'm fine. So goodbye. Go spend Christmas with Ricky."

"Nah, he's been a pain in my ass lately."

"I know the feeling," I say, glaring at him.

"Where's Mason?" he asks, ignoring the implication.

"With Cin."

"Why are you here alone?"

My answer is to glower at him.

"Trouble in paradise?" He chuckles.

Josh isn't far behind me, so when I stop, he runs into my back and I deliver an elbow to his stomach. He grunts, holding his midsection.

"Really? That was uncalled for."

I place the gun on the counter before rummaging through the refrigerator.

"What are you doing?"

"Exactly what the fuck it looks like."

"Let's grab some lunch."

"No thanks."

"If you go, I'll be out of your hair in a week tops. But if you refuse I may stay in Florida until spring."

I swing the fridge shut. "Okay, you win. I'll be showered and dressed in twenty."

He gives me a thumbs-up.

ART

I'm unable to enjoy the big juicy steak, baked potato, and broccoli on my plate because my mind keeps drifting to her.

"She's screwing with you again," Josh says around a mouthful of seafood Alfredo.

"Close your mouth while you chew, you fucking heathen," I growl.

"She has a leash around that thick neck of yours and is leading you around like a lost puppy."

"I'm going to kick your ass up and down this restaurant if you keep yapping."

"Man, drop her like a bad habit."

"I can't."

"Yeah, you can." He takes a bite of garlic bread.

"She's pregnant."

"You're kidding me," he says in disbelief.

"And we're getting married."

Josh gulps down the remainder of his wine, then slams the glass on the table. "You forgave her?"

"No."

"Wow, marrying a girl you don't trust. I'm sure you'll have a long-lasting marriage," he says sarcastically.

"I love her."

Josh peruses me speculatively, surprised by my admission.

"I wish I didn't, but goddamn it, I do."

"Oh fuck." He rubs the back of his neck. "I knew this day was coming the moment I saw her in your damn penthouse, though I hoped it never would."

I squint at him. "If you've got something to say, fucking say it."

"It was me who gave away your secret, not Cin."

"Fuck you say?" My hands form fists, ready to throw down.

"Then, I was holding onto hope my mother would eventually come home, so it was hard to cope when Missy and Cin moved in. I wanted them gone."

Our fathers selected worthless women to sire children with, and we've both suffered because of it.

"My feelings for Cin grew. You see, you're not the only broken boy she helped. I fell for her hard, but she and Trevor started dating. I backed off because he was my best friend."

My anger increases as his story unfolds. My need to hear the conclusion is the only thing keeping me seated.

"Jealousy ate at me, so I ratted you out. If I couldn't have her, neither could you."

"But who told you about my cutting and the cocaine?" His story isn't adding up.

"I overheard you and Cin talking in the kitchen after school on Cole's birthday. That's how I found out everything—you buying cocaine from Bane, Cin catching you in the dining room, and the cutting. Later that night I went looking for evidence and found the baggie under the table."

"Why wait to tell Ricky?"

"I felt bad for letting you take the blame for stealing the truck alone. Not telling Dad was my way of making amends, but we had a precarious relationship, so I kept the baggie to use against you if needed."

"And you searched my bedroom for the razor?"

"I did. I found it in the top drawer."

"You let me hate her for years instead of being a fucking man and owning up to your bullshit."

"Damn right. You're King Grudge, dude. You don't let shit go. We were in a good place and there was no chance in hell I was going to ruin it. Not for her. I thought she was out of our lives for good."

I'm on Josh the next second, knocking him from his chair. Shocked gasps resound throughout the restaurant.

"I'm sorry."

"Not good enough." I jerk him up by his shirt and throw him onto a nearby table. The occupants scream and scramble for cover.

"Fight back!" I yell.

He rights himself. "No."

I tackle him, sending us both crashing through the big glass window. I come to my senses and push to my feet first.

"Get the fuck out of Florida before I commit first-degree murder." I wave towards the broken window. "And you're paying for this."

I have to devise a plan to lure Cin away from her guardians. It's not my fault Josh didn't speak up until now. She's not perfect. We'll both need to get over the past and focus on our future.

Cin

After some convincing, Anneli picked Mom and the boys up and left for North Carolina without me. They're afraid Art will find out I'm home by myself, but I alleviated their fears by promising to stay inside and keep my car in the garage. Visiting family in a sour mood wouldn't be fair to anyone. I'm not very jovial this holiday season. I'd rather wallow in sorrow alone. The pain of losing Art has knocked me on my ass. For the most part, I spend my days crying. I try to put on a strong face for Sebastian and Mason, but it hasn't been easy. More than a few times I've stopped myself from calling him. I miss Art so damn much. It hurts to be with him, and it hurts to be without him, so either way I'm fucking screwed. My soul whispers to me that we're two pieces of one unit and cannot be separated, but my mind says the exact opposite. Logically speaking, we make as much sense as an antelope and a lion being together. Ultimately, one is destined to kill the other. I'm also horny all the time.

When the house has settled down for the night and all is quiet, I slide my hands between my thighs, imagining his mouth on my clit. It just scratches the surface of my itch, nowhere near sating my carnal needs. Though I've been lying in bed since sunset, I'm wide awake. Sleep eludes me. It's become a luxury hard to come by these days.

Finally, I begin to doze off to sleep, but a creaking sound startles me. Sitting up, I glance towards the doorway.

Get a grip, Cin. You're hearing things because you're tired and this is the first time you've stayed the night in the house on your own.

Suddenly, a figure shrouded in darkness enters my bedroom. Alarmed, I leap from the bed and scream at the top of my lungs.

"Calm down." Art's deep timbre washes over me, sending shivers coursing down my spine.

I click on the lamp, and my eyes eagerly eat him up. He's dressed in all black. His T-shirt clings to impressive muscles, and jeans encase his strong legs. "What the fuck are you doing here?"

"Claiming what's mine."

My treacherous pussy throbs, betraying me. God… his words make me want to lie down and spread open for him. But I won't fall under his spell.

"I'm not yours." I backpedal as he advances.

"Your nipples tell the truth while your mouth speaks lies." Art reaches out and rubs a taut nipple through my thin cami top. "Your body knows who it belongs to."

I bite my bottom lip, moaning in ecstasy from his simple touch.

"You've hidden from me for nearly three weeks. That's how long you'll be on your back, getting fucked."

The wall stops my retreat. He dips his head into the crook of my neck, grinding his heavy erection against me while licking along my rapidly beating pulse.

"No," I whisper, pushing him back, accomplishing the feat only because he lets me.

"Is that your final answer?"

"Yes."

"Do you think I'm going to accept that?"

"You have to."

"Wrong." He holds up a syringe.

Reacting instantaneously, I elbow him in the face and a battle ensues. I'm wrestled to the bed, quickly subdued by his powerful thighs straddling my chest and pinning my arms to the sides.

"What is that?" I whimper, feeling a prick in my upper right shoulder. "What have you done?" My words slur, the drug injected into me already taking effect.

"Shhh… go to sleep. The fun will begin soon."

Cin

I open my eyes, noticing two things immediately. First, I'm lying naked on a bed, and second, the gentle rocking beneath me means I'm no longer on land. There is no blanket covering me, leaving me exposed.

Peering to the left, I find Art sitting in a chair, watching me—only a towel hiding his nakedness.

"Where have you taken me?"

"We're still in Florida, but you're on my yacht."

"It's against the law to drug and kidnap people."

"We'll talk later. Now, we fuck."

Art stands, letting the towel fall to his feet. My cunt clenches involuntarily, wetting, preparing itself for his entry. In the middle of the ocean, there's no escaping him. I'm his prisoner. No one will hear my screams for mercy. I'm in mortal danger, yet my mouth waters, remembering his wild fucking and yearning for another taste of him. Only he can quench my thirst. The lustful glint in his eyes and feral expression unnerve me. They hold a promise of pain and pleasure. He'll smash the brick wall I built to pieces and I'm powerless to stop him, but I refuse to lie down and take it. Bring on the rain and the fucking thunder. It's about to be World War III in this motherfucker.

I roll to my stomach, planning to dart across the bed and run from the cabin. To where? No clue, I haven't thought that far ahead. Art grabs my ankles, roughly flips me over, and drags me towards him. He descends to his knees beside the low bed.

"No!" I twist and squirm, aiming to sever his hold.

He propels forward, violently ramming into my tight channel. We shudder, electricity flowing from him into me, rendering us both breathless.

"If you didn't want me between your legs, your pussy wouldn't have yielded so easily or be so warm and welcoming," he murmurs. "It gobbled my dick up, inviting Daddy home for an extended stay."

"Fuck you." My pride halts me from surrendering to the inevitable. I strike out, but Art restrains my right wrist while using his free hand to squeeze my throat.

I utilize my unsecured hand to decorate his skin in lacerations, but he's not fazed. He has his prize and will not be deterred from claiming it. He begins moving, ruthlessly hammering between my thighs, bordering on barbaric. I wrap my legs around his waist, because fuck it, he's won. Shamelessly, I offer his victory on a silver platter, admitting failure. Art jerks me upwards, putting us face-to-face. I place my feet on the floor, spreading my legs wider. This position allows for more movement and I use it to my advantage. I peer into his eyes while circling my hips, meeting his soul-shattering thrusts. The sounds of sex invade my senses, thumping to the beat of my heart. He seizes the back of my head and jaw in a bruising hold.

"If you ever think to deny me again, I'll tie your ass to the fucking bed and that's where you'll stay," he snarls against my mouth.

Our lips connect and we feast on each other's tongues—sucking, nipping, and biting. I cling to him, afraid if I lose my grip I'll be shaken, torn, battered, and severed in half. He bellows at the same time I disintegrate into a million pieces.

"I'm going to fuck you all night," he says, hardening again.

When he's done, I'll need painkillers and stitches.

ART

It's almost five o'clock and Cin hasn't stirred once. I checked on her twice to ensure she was breathing. She has yet to recover from our fuck fest. During the night I became a mindless animal, void of emotion except for the driving need to come inside the depths of her cunt over and over again. Yeah, I tore her ass up, and she's getting the same treatment tonight. She begged me to stop repeatedly, but her pleas fell on deaf ears as I continued to ferociously pulverize her pussy. Her cries spurred me on, increasing my savagery. The sounds of sex make the best fucking harmony. Cin lay defenseless while I gorged myself on her body, but she made sure I wasn't left unscathed. My face, arms, and chest are covered in scratches. One would think I had an unfortunate altercation with an angry alley cat. We found slumber just as the sun brightened the sky. I'm nowhere near close to being finished with her. I have almost three weeks' worth of fucking to catch up on. For now, I'll let her rest so she can replenish her energy.

I reacted swiftly after receiving intel from Logan that Cin did not leave for North Carolina. The perfect opportunity to steal her away presented itself, and I wasn't going to miss it. My yacht was the best place to bring her. She can't run away or attract attention for help. The drug worked fast, putting her to sleep in seconds. I packed her a small bag and was ready to go in under ten minutes. Getting Cin out of the house was the tricky part. A man carrying an unconscious woman would arouse anyone's suspicions. To avoid having the police on my ass, I recruited Logan to be the lookout. He had reservations until zeros were added to his check. Then committing a felony became okay, but he wanted assurances I wouldn't murder her. I tried to alleviate his fears by telling him the only thing I planned on murdering was her pussy, but my declaration had the opposite effect and increased his trepidation. He even called earlier to confirm she's alive.

After waking, I went on deck for fresh air and exercise before showering. Land is visible in the distance but far enough away that attempting to swim it would be a death sentence. I'm at the booth-like table, playing solitaire to keep from boredom. Cin will be famished when she wakes. With that thought in mind, I undertake the task of starting dinner. How hard could it be to prepare a simple meal? More complicated than I assumed, I discover a half hour later. The fish is chewy and tough. Shit, I should've left the cooking to Cin. The salad will have to suffice unless she cooks something to pair with it. I can't risk trying my luck again. Food is scarce since I didn't have adequate time to grocery shop for our staycation. I hear movement in the cabin. The reason for—or maybe she's the bane of—my existence, has risen. She's going to come out guns blazing. Outwardly, I maintain a calm persona, but inwardly I rejoice for the next round of Fuck Cin. I walk back over to the table and resume playing solitaire.

Thirty-five

Cin

I come to, discombobulated and sore. Art fucked me endlessly, a machine focused on annihilation. He brutalized my body, not affording me one moment's respite. Any more of this and I'll need physical therapy. Hours or days might have passed. I'm not sure which. I don't recall falling asleep. Moving to a sitting position takes considerable effort. I rub my gritty eyes and glance around the spacious cabin before leaving the bed, cautiously standing on feeble legs. The engagement ring once again adorns my finger. I limp to the bathroom, desperately needing to empty my bladder. I catch a glimpse of my reflection in the mirror and I'm horrified by what I see. Wild hair, black splotches dotting my cream-colored skin, and dark circles under my eyes—I resemble a zombie. Vivid images from last night permeate my mind, taking center stage. My pussy clenches as I remember screams, grunts, sweaty entangled limbs, and soaked sheets. I touch between my thighs, feeling the stickiness of his dried cum. After relieving myself, I walk back into the room and grab the sheet to hide my nakedness. I open the door, but Art's head remains bent, pretending to be engrossed in his game.

"Look at me, you coldhearted snake!" I yell.

His gaze travels languidly up my body until our eyes meet. "Oh, you're awake." He smiles, showing perfect white teeth. "Did you sleep well?"

"You can't keep me here against my will."

"I cooked dinner for you."

"My mom and Anneli are going to worry when they don't hear from me."

"I have your cell and took the liberty of sending them texts on your behalf." His smug expression boils my blood. "They're expecting a call soon. I'm sure you'll behave and not ruin their trip by telling them about your current situation, but to play it safe the speaker will be on during the conversation."

"You're going to keep me here until they come back, then what?"

Ignoring my question, he goes to the kitchen area and brings back two plates of food. "The fish is overcooked."

"Arthur! How do you think this is going to end?"

"Come eat."

"I'm not hungry." Of course my stomach chooses this moment to growl.

"Doesn't sound like it to me." He smirks. "You can either eat or we can fuck. The choice is yours."

Begrudgingly, I amble over to the table and sit. My vagina needs to recuperate before any sexual activity can resume.

"It was Josh."

"What?"

"He overheard us talking and blabbed to Ricky." Art digs into his salad. "He'll get what's coming to him."

It's a relief to finally be exonerated. "Let it go."

"I'll have my revenge."

"No, this cycle has to stop."

"You should hate him."

"What good has hating someone ever done for you?"

"I can't forgive and forget."

"The past should stay where it is."

"A transgression, no matter when it occurred, has consequences."

"He's your cousin, your blood. How long do you plan on holding this over his head?"

"Anyone who crosses me will face my wrath, including family."

"Does the same go for your children?"

His eyes narrow to slits. "It's called tough love. Hard lessons must be learned. I'm not raising entitled brats."

"I won't have my baby around you."

"It's our baby."

"Are you sure? Not too long ago you weren't."

"Adrian set the record straight."

"You trust his word over mine," I say, hurt.

"Now that the truth is known we can move on."

"Just like that, huh?" He's unbelievable.

"Yes."

"You tied me to your bed and fucked another woman in front of me."

"It's not the end of the world."

I dash up the steps, incensed by his words. Art follows behind me slowly, knowing I have nowhere to run. When he appears, I pull the ring from my finger and pitch it into the ocean. "I'll never marry you."

"You will," he vows, wrestling me to the deck floor.

"No!"

He tears the sheet from me and has his dick inside me in less than thirty seconds.

"Stop!"

Art ravages my body, fucking me so mercilessly with each stroke I slide up the deck. I shake my head from side to side to avoid his lips. In true Art fashion, he clasps my jaw, forcing me to accept his kisses. My disloyal pussy wets for him, greedily supping on his thick manhood. He climbs to his feet, still planted deep in my center, and carries me down the stairs. He lays me on the table, latching onto my hips, and continues his assault.

"Your little stunt means nothing," he grunts. "A ring can easily be replaced."

My climax rocks me to the core, leaving me dazed.

"Fuck, babe, my dick is bathed in your sweet juices," he groans, dropping on top of me.

Once the pleasure recedes, reality sets in. This is so fucking deranged.

"I can't live like this!" Shuddering sobs rack my body.

Art sits down, pulling me onto his lap.

"We aren't setting a good example for Sebastian and Mason," I say. "Our relationship isn't going to work if we constantly fight like cats and dogs. That's not fair to them."

"I'm not giving you up." He grabs my chin and lifts my face to his. "If the conversation is headed in that direction, shut it the fuck down."

"This is not a partnership. It's tyranny. You demand control over every aspect of my life."

"And once you give it to me, we'll be floating on cloud fucking nine."

"I'm not your goddamn lap dog."

"Yes, you are, and you'll obey me or be punished."

"You said you love me, but this isn't love."

"This is how I love."

"Your love hurts."

"I'm a jealous, possessive son of a bitch. That's not going to change."

"Do you want me to grow to resent you? To hate you?"

"I can live with your hate."

"You're a replica of your grandfather."

His mouth forms a thin line.

"We can't bring those boys into a toxic environment. They'll hate us, just like you hated your parents." I definitely hit a nerve.

"My life would be different if it weren't for Josh."

"It's not too late to change."

"What's running through that mind of yours?" he asks.

"There are three things I need from you."

"Name them."

"Forgive Josh, take me home now, and give me space."

"Josh can kiss my ass, I'm not taking you home, and you already had your space."

"I'm filing a restraining order against you," I say quietly. "I'm sorry, but you won't see reason and compromise."

Art gathers my messy hair into a high ponytail, then yanks my head back. "If it wasn't for Sebastian, I would've locked your ass up weeks ago." Anger shines in his turbulent green eyes. "You have no say in what goes down between Josh and me. I'm not done blowing your pussy out, so here is where you'll stay until New Year's Day. I'm not accustomed to being denied what's mine, but I'll give you space for a limited time."

He offers very little, but it's better than nothing at all.

Four months later

Cin

After the fuckathon on the yacht, Art kept his distance for a week, then the fighting and fucking commenced. He called my bluff and won. I never had any intention on getting a restraining order against him, which royally pissed off Mom and Anneli to no end. They couldn't babysit forever, so Art and I fell into the same routine—though he's not as intense as before due to my growing belly. I haven't told them what caused the major fallout between Art and me, and I never will. True to his word, he bought me another ring, and he has not exonerated Josh for his deceit. We aren't married and still live separately. He gave me until the birth of our baby to come to terms with the way things are going to be, or he's dragging me down the aisle kicking and screaming.

The man is fucking stubborn, but his hard exterior slipped during the second sonogram, and it was magnificent to see. His gaze stayed riveted on the monitor. It was true love—a sight to behold. When the ultrasound tech announced we were having a baby girl, Art smiled—a rare genuine look of pure joy. She has him wrapped around her little finger and she hasn't even been born yet. Rubbing and laying his head on my protruding midsection has become his favorite pastime. He stares in awe whenever our baby moves inside me. There's no question Art will do anything in his power to keep her safe, even forfeiting his own life.

For the tenth time in two minutes, I reposition myself on the pregnancy pillow Art gifted me. I'm unsuccessful in finding a comfortable position. At six months pregnant, I'm bigger than normal, and I've been experiencing lower back pain. It's time to get up to cook dinner anyway, and I promised Sebastian and Mason we'd bake cookies. I roll out of the bed and waddle into the hall. As I descend the stairs, a toy car catches my attention, but it's too late to avoid it. I step on it and lose my balance, causing me to tumble down the stairs.

Thinking the worst, I rush to the hospital after receiving a call from Missy about Cin's fall. I park directly in front of the entrance. Not willing to waste any time getting to her side, I leave the car door open and the engine running. I race from the elevator and down the hall where I spot Missy and Anneli. They're both crying.

God, please. I am not a praying man, but please have mercy on me.

"Where is she?" I ask in a broken voice.

"She has to have an emergency Cesarean section," Anneli answers.

"Cin's asking for you," Missy says. "Only one person can be in the operating room."

"The doctor is coming," Anneli says.

I anxiously watch him approach.

"Hello, I'm Dr. Channing." He holds out his hand. "I'm assuming you're the father."

"Yes," I reply, shaking his hand.

"Surgery is in five minutes. We need to get you prepped."

"Will our baby live?" I hold my breath, waiting for a response.

"Ms. Belo suffered a partial placental abruption, causing internal bleeding and depriving the baby of oxygen."

"What are their chances for survival?" I ask, feeling sick to my stomach.

"It's hard to say. Ms. Belo will be given a transfusion during the procedure to replace lost blood, and a pediatric team is on standby to provide care for your daughter the moment she's taken from the womb. You have my word everything possible is being done to ensure mother and child survive."

I embrace Missy, then Anneli. "Cin is strong. She'll pull through and bring our baby with her." I follow the doctor down the hall and suit up before entering the operating room.

"Art," she says weakly, giving me a small smile.

I walk over and kiss her on the forehead. "I'm here, baby."

The surgery starts promptly. I whisper words of encouragement, remaining calm for her sake though I'm actually scared out of my mind. Minutes blend together until finally I catch a glimpse of a small body being pulled from the incision. Our precious girl is blue and limp, so tiny she could fit in the palm of my hand.

Doctors begin to work on her immediately. "Starting neonatal resuscitation."

"Is she out?" Cin asks, fear shining in her eyes. "Why isn't she crying?"

"It's okay. They're working on her." I struggle to hold tears at bay, needing to put on a brave face for Cin.

"Her Apgar score is low," a doctor says.

"What does that mean?" she sobs. "I want to see her now."

Suddenly, her head lolls to the side, then a loud beep resounds in the room.

"Patient flatlined."

"Cin!" I shout.

"Please step back," Dr. Channing says.

Becoming hysterical will only hinder the doctors in their efforts to resuscitate Cin, so I give them a wide berth. My world is cracking, soon to implode on itself. I drop to my knees and do something I've never done in my entire life. I pray.

Five months later

ART

Five months ago, my soul mate died. I cursed God and beseeched him to give her back. She lost more blood than expected, sending her body into shock. It took three fucking minutes for doctors to revive her, but I swear it felt like hours. The team had to work extra hard to resuscitate our daughter, but almost twenty minutes later, her piercing cry reverberated through the operating room. Cin was released six days later. In the weeks following the birth, Cin and I lived in a nightmare. We decided to forgo selecting a name, instead choosing to focus on our baby's health. It was hell not knowing from one day to the next if she would survive. The hospital became a second home for us.

Sebastian blamed himself for leaving the toy car on the step and started having trouble sleeping. Being no stranger to insomnia, I made it a priority to put his mind at ease.

Both of our families pulled together, offering unwavering support. Revenge for Josh's deception was put on hold. The old man, Ricky, Katrina, and Lilah came to visit. Even Anneli and I came to a truce. Our daughter's diagnosis improved as the weeks went on, and we finally chose a name—Arabella Elise King. She's beautiful, the most precious thing I've ever beheld. She's a mixture of us both. Arabella's eyes are a green and hazel blend and her hair is black and wavy. I ordered Cin to pack and move in with me pronto, not caring that my command angered her. I refuse to live separately from my daughter. She deserves to be brought into a household where both parents are present. Sebastian has settled into his bedroom and the nursery is done. It'll be awhile before she's mobile, but the entire mansion is already childproof. Four months to the day Arabella entered the world, she was discharged. I gave Cin thirty days to plan our wedding. The task was accomplished with the help of her mother and Anneli. We're not ready to leave Arabella, so the honeymoon is being postponed.

It's our wedding day. Forty guests are in attendance. I never thought I'd be a jittery groom, but here I am, nervous as fuck. An enlarged photograph of Cole is stationed to the left of me. This day wouldn't be complete without him. The doors of the church open and I'm in awe at the sight before me. Cin is wearing a simple veil and an off-white knee-length dress. She didn't go the traditional route. She chose to walk down the aisle with Arabella in her arms and the boys walking alongside her. Our family is finally whole. The ceremony is short, and after the photographer takes pictures, we head to the Falcon.

Cin

Today is like a dream. Uncertainty has filled me for the last year, but finally I'm optimistic about the future. I'm all smiles, mingling with family and friends.

Josh ambles up beside me. "Can I talk to you privately?"

"Sure."

We walk over to an empty table and sit.

"I'm sorry for not speaking up." He takes a breath. "It was a shitty thing for me to do."

"Josh, it's okay."

"I'd be pissed if I were you."

"Grudges are a waste of time."

"Hopefully your mindset will rub off on your husband."

I laugh. "One can hope."

"What's so funny?" Art appears at my side.

"Oh, nothing," I snicker.

"Josh, do you mind if I dance with my wife?"

"Not at all."

Art grasps my hand and leads me to the middle of the banquet hall. We wrap our arms around each other and sway to the music.

"You're due for a spanking later."

"What?" I ask, astounded.

"Well, you were talking to Josh and you know the rules."

"The arrangement ended months ago."

"The rules will always apply."

"I'm your wife now."

"And I'm still a jealous motherfucker."

"You're seriously going to ruin our wedding day?"

"It's your fault for flirting and joking with Josh."

"Expect a fight."

"Am I supposed to be deterred?" He smiles smugly.

"Okay, bring it on," I challenge.

A mischievous glint flashes in his eyes. "I was hoping you'd say that."

Epilogue

Cin

All is right in my universe. Sometimes Art shakes shit up, but overall, I'm content. I have an amazing family. My husband and best friend are getting along. Mom even found love again, with Ricky no less. That news was a bombshell to everyone. Apparently, they reconnected when she visited North Carolina last December. Their rekindled romance came to light after the wedding. She's even contemplating relocating to be with him. It'll surely be difficult not having her near, but she deserves happiness. My selfishness destroyed their relationship once before, but I refuse to let history repeat itself. I freely gave her my blessing. I'll talk to her on the phone every day and visit often. Hopefully, wedding bells will be in her near future.

Arabella is a daddy's girl. She's the light of Art's life. The chick is spoiled rotten—definitely a diva in the making because of her indulgent father. Playing an active role in our children's lives is important to Art, so he works from home most days to make that possible. He puts them above all else, not wanting them to ever feel the empty void he felt as a child. In regard to Art and me… well, he is and will always be a domineering jackass. I've come to terms with it. If it's not him keeping me up all damn night, it's our daughter. I smile, recalling last night's sexual escapades when Art enters our bedroom.

"It's time."

I sit cross-legged in the middle of the bed folding laundry. "I'm busy."

"Oh no, you've been making excuses all week. Get your ass up."

"We can't leave the kids home alone."

"I called your mother, who happily agreed to come over and watch them. She's already here. Meet me out front in ten minutes."

Oh fuck.

ART

I lean against my Ducati Multistrada, waiting for Cin to appear. She has an unnatural fear of motorcycles. It took weeks to convince her to go on a ride with me. She relented when I promised never to ask again if she agreed. I'm positive she'll enjoy the outing and request more. I never imagined I'd be married with three kids. Life has a funny way of throwing curve balls. I no longer feel guilty about being happy. In my heart I know Cole would want that for me. There isn't a day that goes by where he doesn't enter my thoughts. He'll always be remembered.

Cin storms outside, looking none too happy.

"Turn that frown upside down."

"Eat shit."

"Is that any way to talk to your loving husband?" I chide.

"I survived birth to die in a motorcycle crash," she mumbles.

"Being a little dramatic, are we?" I ask, handing her a helmet. I have one of my own too. After Mason was born, I started taking precautions when riding.

"Why is this important to you?"

"I want to share my joy of riding with you," I answer and softly kiss her lips. "Do you trust me?"

"As much as I trust a rattlesnake."

"Ouch."

She lays her head on my chest. "I trust you."

"Good." I climb onto the bike. "Hop on."

She settles in behind me and we're off. It's cliché as fuck, but we ride off into the sunset.

Thank you for reading

The ride has finally concluded, hopefully you enjoyed it and look forward to more of my possessive domineering assholes! Don't forget to leave a review and read my other books! Connect with me on social media:

Facebook – Author Lorrain Allen

Instagram – author_lorrain_allen

TikTok – authorlorrainallen

Twitter – AuthorLAllen

About the author

Lorrain Allen currently resides on the East Coast. She has one amazing, albeit spoiled, son. She loves to get away from the world by losing herself in a book. Her long-term goal is to pen dark, erotic, paranormal, contemporary, new adult, and young adult romances. The subject matters of her books are controversial, but what's life without a little controversy?

Standalones

Slippery When Wet: When Adults Play

The Games We Play

Consumed: A Dark Stalker Age Gap Romance

Maverick's Madness: A Dark High School Bully Romance

Living in Cin Duet

When Art Rises: Living in Cin (A Dark High School Romance)

When Art Falls: Living in Cin (A Dark Romance)

A Little Taste of Sin Series

Sweet Peach

Midas Touch

Gods of Ruin MC Series

Beautiful Hate: A Dark MC Romance

www.authorlorrainallen.com

Printed in Great Britain
by Amazon